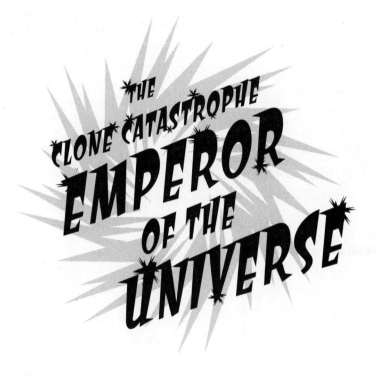

STARSCAPE BOOKS
BY DAVID LUBAR

DAVID LUBAR

THE
CLONE CATASTROPHE
EMPEROR
OF THE
UNIVERSE

STARSCAPE

A TOM DOHERTY ASSOCIATES BOOK
NEW YORK

THE CLONE CATASTROPHE: EMPEROR OF THE UNIVERSE

Copyright © 2021 by David Lubar

A Starscape Book
Published by Tom Doherty Associates
120 Broadway
New York, NY 10271

www.tor-forge.com

The Library of Congress Cataloging-in-Publication Data
is available upon request.

ISBN 978-1-250-18933-2 (paper over board)
ISBN 978-1-250-18934-9 (ebook)

Our books may be purchased in bulk for promotional, educational, or business use. Please contact your local bookseller or the Macmillan Corporate and Premium Sales Department at 1-800-221-7945, extension 5442, or by email at MacmillanSpecialMarkets@macmillan.com.

First Edition: April 2021

Printed in the United States of America

0 9 8 7 6 5 4 3 2 1

FOR SCIENCE

BEFORE WE BEGIN

Welcome back!

Your return pleases me.

I assume you are returning, and not diving in cold, without any knowledge of what has already happened. If you haven't read the breathtaking account of how Nicholas V. Landrew of Yelm, Washington, became emperor of the universe, some of what follows might seem strange, confusing, or contradictory.

On the other hand—or hoof—even if you've read that account, some of what follows might still seem strange, confusing, or contradictory. That is the nature of reality. Or the reality of nature. Fear not. I will do my best to make things clear.

Speaking of which, I will recount Nicholas's further

adventures in the same manner as before, speaking directly to you here, in these brief illuminations, excursions, and intrusions, but giving myself a bit more narrative distance in the main story.

Essentially, I am Jeef, here. But Jeef is *she* there. You'll get used to it. As have I. But enough about me. Or you. Let us drop in on our emperor, and see how he is faring with his new position in life.

UNBELIEVABLE

Y ou can't make me take out the garbage!" Nicholas screamed. "I'm the emperor of the universe!"

After a long day at school, followed by two hours of homework, and a half hour spent folding and putting away his laundry, his only goal was to grab a snack from the fridge and take it up to his room, where he could relax, play games, and strew crumbs until dinnertime. Instead, he'd been ambushed with the one chore he hated the most. It didn't help that he'd hardly gotten any sleep for the past month.

Still, he hadn't planned to share the news of his exalted position with his parents quite yet. Nicholas clamped his mouth shut at the end of the outburst. His parents stared at him. He stared back, briefly, and then looked around wildly as he realized he'd blurted out the second largest secret on Earth. The first being that humanity was not only far from alone in the universe, but also far, far, far from being special, unique, or dominant in any way. Earth was, at best, a speck of dust.

Nicholas unclamped his mouth and attempted to explain the inexplicable. "I . . . um . . . I wasn't . . ." He glanced down at his pocket for guidance, but his sentient and highly articulate gerbil, Henrietta, just sniffed her nose and tilted her head slightly to the side, as if to say, *You dug this hole. You fill it.*

"Too many superhero movies," his mom said to his dad.

"Too many comic books," his dad said to his mom.

"Too many video games," they both said, in a pleasing harmony of voices they'd honed from years of singing together onstage as one half of a popular Beatles parody group that performed concerts all around the world.

Nicholas's mom and dad, Melanie and Harrison Landrew to their friends, paused in their parental enumeration of all the usual suspects that could be blamed for unacceptable or overly imaginative behavior to smile at each other in appreciation of this lovely musical moment.

After which, they sighed in unison at the heavy burden of raising a difficult child in this modern world—which seemed to have grown significantly more turbulent during the past month of unexpected gasoline shortages and surging oil prices—and turned their attention back to their one and only offspring. They'd often held private discussions where they theorized that Nicholas's difficulty fitting in with his peers stemmed from a deep core of creativity that would eventually make itself known to the rest of the world.

"Even if you really were the emperor of the universe," his mom said, "you're still our son. What does that make us?"

Nicholas had no idea. He wasn't used to either of his parents offering any sort of argument that resembled a deep thought or a logical construction. As the resident adults of the household, they fell mostly into the *Because we said so* style of parenting. He decided the best response was to keep his mouth shut and take out the garbage. And the best technique for doing so would not be the first one that came to mind—kicking it across the kitchen with enough power and accuracy to send it straight through the window. Given that he generally lacked both power and accuracy in his athletic performances, this was a solid decision.

At least, based on his mom's use of "really were the emperor," it looked like his parents hadn't taken him seriously. That was not exactly a departure from their normal relationship. And it was totally understandable they wouldn't instantly accept what he'd just told them, kneel before him, and turn over the car keys, given that he himself still had trouble, at times, believing he was actually the emperor of the universe.

So he donated his own sigh to the growing level of carbon dioxide in the kitchen atmosphere, acknowledged the inevitable struggle that lay ahead, and prepared for battle with his mortal enemy. Either the garbage can in the kitchen was too big for the plastic bags his parents bought, or the bags were too small for the can. The top of the bag clung to the top of the can like a tourniquet. Whatever the reason for the disparity, every encounter with the task led to frustration, a messy struggle, and at least one bruised finger as he wrestled the bag free of the can. If he'd been offered the choice of taking the garbage out or eating it, he suspected he'd need time to make a decision.

"Stupid garbage," he muttered as he tackled the task.

The garbage has no capacity for thought. It can't be smart or stupid, Jeef said.

Nicholas looked up at the sky. He always stared toward the sky, and outer space, when he spoke with Jeef, even though she was not just up, and her voice didn't seem to come from any particular place. She was everywhere. Though she'd started life as a cow, she'd been atomized in the presence of an antimatter core, which resulted in her becoming spread throughout the universe. She was as much to his left or right as she was over his head. But he needed to think of her in less universal terms when he spoke to her. "Yeah. I know. But it's still stupid." He tied the drawstring on the bag after he'd wrestled it out of the can, and put it in the big bin by the curb. Then, he dragged the empty can back to the house.

His parents didn't mention anything about his outburst when he came inside. During dinner, they mostly talked about whether it was time to replace the carpet in the living room. Nicholas wanted to suggest they replace the kitchen garbage can, but he figured this was not the time to raise that topic and remind them of his claim. By the time the meal ended, he was sure he could go back to his normal routine without fear of discovery.

Nicholas's normal routine was nine parts ordinary,

involving school, homework, family meals, science fiction movies, superhero comics, gaming, and whatever else a twelve-year-old boy does while he waits to reach a more significant age, like thirteen, eighteen, or twenty-one. It was also one part extraordinary, which explained his lack of sleep. For the past month, ever since becoming emperor of the universe, he'd slipped away nearly every night, by means of teleportation, accompanied by his trusted advisor, Henrietta, to romp around alien worlds with his guide, chronicler, and untrusted advisor, Clave. There was a whole lot of universe out there to explore, and the thrill of doing it was still irresistible. Even if he wanted to take a break, his presence was, to state the obvious, universally in demand. And there was only one of him to go around.

Tonight would be no different. After placing his plate and silverware in the dishwasher, he glanced across the kitchen at his parents, who were paying no attention to him, and then headed up to his room to launch himself into that evening's slice of this far-from-ordinary adventure.

When Nicholas reached his room, he flipped up the top of Henrietta's extra-large cage, where the entire adventure had begun, stepped inside, switched on his marvelously modified, perpetually powered cell phone, opened his equally marvelously modified communications app, and sent the message *I'm ready* to Clave. A moment later, as he was engulfed in a flash of purple light, he felt the familiar sensations of teleportation. As always, he was glad to leave Earth behind.

SPARE CHANGE

Despite millions of years of evolution, humans do not cope very well with change. Whether this change comes in the form of something insignificant, like having the muffin section of their supermarket moved to the other side of the deli counter, or from something monumental, such as discovering they are not alone in the universe, and thus most likely not the greatest living things in all of creation, change causes ripples of unease. And, while humans had not yet learned there was highly evolved life on other planets, things had changed in other ways on Earth, thanks to Nicholas.

His removal of all petroleum from the Earth's crust had ended the petro-shielding that screened humans from the Ubiquitous Matrix. Citizens of all nations found they could understand each other without any language barrier. Or, more accurately, they could hear what was being said. Hearing and understanding stood as far apart as ever, with much depending on the willingness of the hearer to accept what the speaker was trying to say, or to even make the effort to truly listen to another being while simultaneously juggling a half dozen self-absorbed thoughts, fears, worries, and wishes. In other words, to use an old Earth saying, the more things change, the more they stay the same.

The removal of all of Earth's petroleum did not go unnoticed, especially in oil-rich nations, though the owners of that petroleum did their best to hide the disappearance as they struggled to figure out what had happened. Oil and its products don't only provide power to turbines and vehicles. They also give enormous political and military power to those who control the supply. The initial fluctuation of gas prices was seen as annoying but not unusual by the general population. Later, as prices surged, annoyance would shift toward anger and panic.

The simultaneous introduction of unlimited free energy would have more than made up for this loss of oil, as Nicholas intended, had the same groups that controlled the petroleum not cornered the supply of several rare-earth elements required for the production of this new technology as soon as they became aware of it. Which, surprisingly, was not all that soon. More about that delay, later. For now, let's get back to Nicholas.

SOCKS? NO SWEAT

"I almost spilled my secret to my parents," Nicholas said when he stepped onto the bridge of Clave's ship, *The Nick of Space*. He set Henrietta down next to the shallow box of newspapers he kept in the corner for her entertainment. She hopped in and started shredding a page with the headline *Governor Launches Probe of Petroleum Prices*.

"I mean, I did spill my secret," Nicholas added, "but they thought I was making stuff up."

Instead of responding, or capturing his usual recording of Nicholas's arrival for later broadcast, Clave held out a bright red ball of fuzzy cloth. "You should change your socks."

"Why?" Nicholas asked. He glanced down at his feet,

but didn't see anything wrong with his current clothing choice.

Clave sniffed. "Trust me. It's a good idea. The Perlaki have a painfully sensitive sense of smell, and are highly offended by any form of mammalian foot odor."

Nicholas had his hand halfway out to grab the offering before he stopped to ask the obvious question. "Perlaki?"

"An aquatic life-form on the planet Perlak. They're at the top of our list for requesting a visit," Clave said.

"What do they want from me?" Nicholas asked.

Clave opened a list on his console and tapped the top line, opening a second document. He scrolled up and down through it several times, mumbled various inaudible phrases, then said, "I can't seem to find that part in my notes. Doesn't matter. It must be important. As I said, they're at the top of the list. They'll fill us in when we get there." He pushed the socks against Nicholas's chest. "Get changed. They're waiting for us."

"The list . . ." Nicholas said, as if he were a French king saying, "The guillotine." An endless stream of individuals, households, towns, cities, continents, planets, solar systems, and galaxies claimed to have an urgent need for the emperor's attention. None of them seemed at all troubled by the fact that the emperor had only recently learned there was other life in the universe, or that the emperor's own life on Earth had begun a mere twelve and three quarters years ago. But his age and inexperience proved not to be much of a problem so far. While the emperor had, among other things, to swear to solve that which couldn't be solved, ever since making that pledge Nicholas hadn't encountered anything much that couldn't be fixed with a bit of common sense.

"I wish I could clone myself," Nicholas said.

"That's easy enough to do," Clave said. "The technology exists. Though it's hard enough civilizing one of you. I couldn't imagine facing a cluster of you."

"I was kidding." Nicholas took the socks from Clave, sat in the co-pilot's seat, and put them on. It did not occur to him to ask how an aquatic life-form would be troubled by odors in the air. Though he himself was troubled by something. "I'm already civilized. I'm just inexperienced. That's different."

"And equally difficult to deal with," Clave said. "Strap in." He took the ship to the nearby jump node. Each node allowed virtually instant transportation to a limited number of nodes throughout the universe. Each of those nodes was similarly connected to other nodes. In theory, a ship could get anywhere by means of enough jumps.

Nicholas counted the jump cubes as they loaded

themselves into the console. There were seven. Each cube enabled a single jump. Nicholas sat back and enjoyed the sensation as the ship made the seven jumps required to reach Perlak. Then he braced himself for the usual jolting ride as Clave navigated the last stretch from the jump node to the planet.

It was a spectacular world, even when seen from far off. Nicholas glanced at it through the viewport, but didn't pay much attention to the scenic vista of purple oceans and luminous clouds that would have made any of his fellow humans gasp. He'd seen so many planets.

"My socks don't smell, do they?" he asked Henrietta. "The ones I took off?"

"Everything smells," she said. "But your socks usually smell like cheese, so I'm not complaining."

"Good cheese or bad cheese?" Nicholas asked. He liked American cheese and cheddar, but his uncle had some cheeses that were full of mold and smelled like they'd come out of another part of the cow that was farther back than the udder.

"They're all good," Henrietta said.

Nicholas decided not to ask what the rest of his wardrobe smelled like. But another question came to mind. "Jeef, can you smell things?"

If I turn my attention to them, she said.

"Do my socks smell?"

I prefer not to find out.

"I guess I can't blame you." Nicholas dropped the subject and turned his attention back to the viewport.

They docked at an orbiting landing station. From there, they took a shuttle to the surface, and then below it. The shuttle went directly into the water. Fifty feet down, it coupled with a chamber that seemed to be made of nothing but air.

"We're in a bubble," Nicholas said as he stepped off the ship. He winced as he realized the air inside smelled like tuna salad that had just started to turn bad enough to make you sick but not so spoiled as to kill you. If he kept his sneakers on for a whole month and took daily strolls through sewage pits, manure piles, and the floors of slaughterhouses, he couldn't imagine his socks would smell even halfway as bad as the current air.

"Yeah. Of course we're in a bubble." Clave pulled out his sfumbler to record a snippet of the meeting to share with his followers. "Otherwise, we'd drown."

"But it's just a *bubble*," Nicholas said. He pushed his foot against the floor at his feet. It felt like the thin plastic Jeef had been wrapped in when he'd first taken her from his refrigerator. That wrapper had become dangerously worn pretty quickly.

Nicholas thought back to the time he'd tried to swim underwater for the entire length of the lap lane in the community pool. He'd barely made it halfway. He'd promised himself he'd work all summer on his breathing, until he could go the full length and all the way back. But he'd never given it a second attempt. At the moment, as he tried to estimate how many lap lengths below the surface they were, he was regretting this lapse.

"Stay in my pocket," he told Henrietta. He shuddered as he imagined her tiny claws puncturing whatever it was that protected them from drowning.

"That's been my plan since we arrived," Henrietta said.

"Relax," Clave said. "They wouldn't endanger the emperor. At least, not intentionally. And a bubble has never collapsed."

"Almost never," someone said in a voice that sounded like it was being spoken through an electric kazoo.

Nicholas spotted a dull yellow fish the size of a manatee, with the head of a frog and more rippling fins than he could easily count, putting its purple lips against the other side of the bubble.

"That makes me feel so much better," he said.

The dozen Perlaki who were there to meet him insisted on honoring him with their traditional greeting dance of the five thousand fins and flippers. The walls of the bubble rippled and danced, too. Nicholas started hyperventilating in preparation for a frantic swim to the surface. This was a tragic mistake, given the current stench in the air.

Fortunately, nobody burst his bubble.

Once the seemingly endless greeting was over, the Perlaki who had already spoken to him introduced itself as Mibble von Algae and praised Nicholas for his lack of foot odor.

"Thank you, I think . . ." Nicholas said. "Why did you ask me here?"

"Our planet is drying up," Mibble said. "Our orbit shifted."

"So all you need is more water?" Nicholas asked.

"That's all," Mibble said.

"Or a return to the original orbit," Nicholas said as he thought about some of the things that could go wrong when elements and compounds were shifted on a planet-wide basis. He forced his mind to shut out the images of entire planets on fire.

"That would work, too," Mibble said.

Nicholas could easily see a dozen other ways to fix that problem. It was hardly rocket science. Though a really enormous rocket could possibly fix the problem. He suggested some more solutions. The Perlaki cheered. He crossed the flimsy floor again and returned to the shuttle—though not before hyperventilating through the seemingly endless Perlaki farewell dance of ten thousand fins, flippers, tails, and gills.

"Why did you even bring me here?" he asked Clave when they took their seats. "Anyone could have taken care of this. It definitely isn't worth getting put at the top of the list. Or even the bottom."

"I misunderstood their need," Clave said. "It's not easy dealing with all the requests we get. And, as you could see, they were not really deep thinkers. They didn't do the greatest job of explaining their need in their request."

As Clave babbled on far too long with excuses, Nicholas examined his face. Something in his voice didn't sound right, but the Menmarian's range of facial expressions, from pure rage to total joy, always showed so little emotion that it was hard to judge his sincerity. Nicholas was glad he'd never have to play poker against him.

ELSEWHERE IN SPACE AND SLIME

When *Cloud Mansion Intergalactic,* the massive spacecraft that served as his home and base of his operations, self-destructed—with a bit of help from Nicholas, Clave, and the Beradaxian singer, Spott—Morglob Sputum, the universally famous Phleghmhackian talent agent, was in his office, near the center of the complex, negotiating a contract with a pair of Cygnian flamenco dancers. Thus, he wasn't ejected into the bleak vacuum of space at a high velocity. It was more of a gentle-but-insistent nudge. Four days later, he was still traveling at pretty much the same speed, since Isaac Newton nailed it when he observed that a body in motion tends to stay in motion unless acted upon by an external force, even if that body happens to resemble an enormous sneeze.

Morglob was basically coasting.

The Gristidian pirate ship he encountered was another matter. It was accelerating at full throttle, racing toward a rumored incapacitated freighter carrying a precious cargo of Swerdlian tongue swords. Morglob met this external force head on—or would have, if his anatomy had contained a discernable head—splorking into it with enough force to smear himself into a thin jelly across several square meters of the outer hull. The ship's captain noticed a glitch in the instrument readout, indicating a minor collision. He ordered a crew member to suit up and examine the hull.

While the crew member was pushing herself into a spacesuit, Morglob was pulling himself back into a thicker form. When the crew member entered the airlock, Morglob was in the process of flowing toward the small hatch on the outside of that same airlock. When the outer hatch cycled open, he splashed inside, startling the crew member, who was in the process of attaching her safety line. She lost her footing and stumbled into space, untethered.

By the time someone thought to check on the drifting crew member, it was far too late to try to find her. Not that they would have made the effort, even if they'd seen her drift past the viewport, waving frantically and trailing her safety line like an umbilical cord. The pirate code of honor specifically forbids honorable acts. Or codes. This is just one of the many reasons why pirates tend to have very short careers.

When the remaining crew members eventually cycled the airlock and admitted Morglob, they formed a circle and stared down at the slimy, glistening creature. "Down" was quite far since the average Gristidian stood around seven feet tall, and nearly all of the crew were above average in that particular category. (The list of traits where they were below average would require far more pages than it merits.)

"What is it?" the first mate asked. He prodded Morglob with his foot.

"Jelly?" the second mate suggested.

"I like jelly," another crew member said, extending a tentative finger halfway toward the red-tinged blob.

As they stood there, discussing the virtues of jelly, along with their perpetual tragic lack of toast, and daring each other to give the currently available jelly a taste, Morglob glorped across the room to an air duct. It wouldn't work as well as his normal speaking tube, but it would have to do. He flowed around it and said, "Bring your captain here."

The pirates stared at each other. The captain had just retreated to his cabin for a nap. They argued among themselves about whose turn it was to wake him.

"Now!" Morglob shouted.

Losing his home had made him cranky. The long drift through space afterward had not improved his mood. It had, however, given him ample time to contemplate various means of revenge against the monsters who had destroyed his home. They would pay. And they would suffer. He did not know, yet, of the events that had transpired after he was booted into space. He had no idea Nicholas the Betrayer, as he thought of that ungrateful biped, was now the emperor of the universe.

Morglob would learn this soon enough, since Nicholas seemed to be a favorite subject of newscasts, sfumbles, and reality series. That information would make his task far more simple, since an emperor would be a lot easier to find than a quisling little human. As would his companions, the treacherous Beradaxian, Spott, who had showed no appreciation for the steady job Morglob had given him, and the insufferable amateur sfumbler, Clam or Craig or whatever his name was, who also needed to be punished.

Morglob chuckled, producing a sound best described as a small wet fart made by someone sitting in a mud puddle, when he realized this recent event would make their eventual destruction all that much more enjoyable, since they would fall from great heights—figuratively, for sure, as well as literally, if it could be arranged. Morglob issued further glorbles of happiness as he pulled free of the register and awaited the captain, who, if all went according to Morglob's rapidly forming plan, would soon lose his position of power, as well as something much more precious. The sound caused the pirates within earshot to glance nervously at the seat of their own pants.

"The betrayers will suffer," Morglob said. "And then they will die."

He was currently unaware that he was not the only one with plans of vengeance. He'd learn about this, too, soon enough.

OUTCLASSED

One month ago, on the day Nicholas returned to school after being crowned emperor of the universe, he'd seen, for the first time, the alluring Stella Galendrea, the much-younger cousin of his algebra teacher and a fairly perfect embodiment of his ideal girl. She looked like a seventh-grade version of the enthralling newscaster, Stella Astrallis, with hair only slightly less flowing, eyes only slightly less dazzling, and a nose only slightly less cute.

The newscaster had been designed by computer scientists and psychologists to appear to each person as their ideal partner. She was irresistible to anyone who wasn't totally self-absorbed. Nicholas's classmate, on the other hand, had been designed by nature and genetics. And yet they could have been drawn by the same hand. After all that he'd experienced during the adventures that led up to him becoming emperor, Nicholas was no longer troubled by coincidences. He just viewed the good ones as gifts, and the bad ones as cosmic mistakes.

As for the flesh-and-blood Stella, every time Nicholas had tried to start a conversation with her—which was pretty much every time they were within three feet of each other—he'd experience a curious physical phenomenon not unlike the law of conservation of energy or the balancing of an equation. When he opened his mouth to utter even a single-syllable greeting, his throat closed down proportionally. It was as if his tongue and larynx were wired together. He was fairly sure if he opened his mouth as wide as possible, his throat would shut down completely, and he would suffocate. Fortunately, he was also vaguely aware that a hugely gaping mouth was not his best look.

It was not surprising, given Nicholas's limited communication skills, that nothing much changed on a daily basis. But two weeks ago, as Nicholas was heading out of algebra, Stella demonstrated that her own vocal components were not wired in the same debilitating manner.

"Hi," she said.

Nicholas's brain responded by briefly becoming as empty as the space between galaxies, after which it flooded with an abundance of clashing thoughts.

I'm the emperor of the universe, Nicholas told himself after he'd regained partial control of his brain, in an attempt to find enough courage to respond. That helped.

He bolstered himself a bit more.

I've traveled across the universe and cheated death.

That reinforcement of his self-image enabled him to gasp out a version of "hi" that, though lacking in a good portion of its initial consonant, did convey the required long vowel sound. Though, as far as length, it was on the short side of long.

"You're kind of quiet," Stella said.

Nicholas nodded. He really couldn't argue with that. His brain gave him a clever response—*I can only agree by making that statement untrue,* which sounded like something Jeef would say. His mouth wisely refused to take part in this and remained closed. On the positive side, his throat continued to allow air to flow to his lungs, and from there to his brain.

Stella stared at him, as if expecting him to take a more active role in the conversation.

Say something! Nicholas gave himself an order, but failed to obey it. One tiny portion of his brain wandered off to contemplate the irony of the emperor disobeying his own command, but the remainder was still locked in semi-paralysis.

Stella issued the tiniest of sighs. "Well, I need to get—"

Before she could hit the last word of that sentence, her eyes widened slightly, and her gaze dropped to Nicholas's chest. Or, more accurately, his shirt pocket.

He glanced down, too, knowing there could have been only one thing that would draw her attention to that exact spot. Henrietta was peering out. She'd placed her adorable paws on the edge of the pocket and lifted her adorable head high enough so her adorable pink ears were visible.

Don't scream, Nicholas thought, as he continued his silent part of the conversation.

Happily his highly stereotyped fear that Stella would be terrified of mice, like most highly stereotypical fears, was unfounded. Her expression of surprise flowed into a smile of delight that was, itself, delightful.

"How cute," she said.

Nicholas was vaguely aware that students were flowing past the two of them, leaving algebra behind and moving into the hallway toward the next precisely metered segment of their education.

Stella extended her hand toward Henrietta. "May I?"

Henrietta and Nicholas both nodded.

Stella skritched Henrietta gently on the head with one pink-painted nail. "How cute. What's her name?"

"Henrietta," Nicholas said.

"That's a pretty name. Why is she here?"

"She likes algebra," Nicholas said. He wasn't sure where that answer had come from. Though Henrietta had never given him any reason to believe that she disliked that branch of math, or any other. So it wasn't really a lie.

Stella smiled, and then laughed. "That's funny. But I can't blame her. Algebra is great."

Nicholas wasn't sure whether to respond to that with a laugh of his own. But Stella didn't seem to be joking. And they'd actually had an exchange of words that resembled a normal conversation.

After giving Henrietta a second skritch and a parting

pat, Stella headed off. If the ball was now in his court, Nicholas had no idea how to proceed. He wasn't even sure what sport they were metaphorically playing.

"I wish I had an older brother," he whispered to Henrietta. "I could use some advice."

"You have the universe at your fingertips," she said.

"Yeah. But a Rigelean or a Panaxpolivan isn't going to have a clue about how an Earth boy asks an Earth girl out for a date." He paused to marvel at how many alien races he knew about. It definitely wasn't a small world, after all.

"Good point," Henrietta said. "You could ask Clave. He's fairly humanoid. And older."

"His people like to eat their own children," Nicholas said. "I suspect there might also be other differences, large and small, between Menmarians and humans."

"Another good point," Henrietta said. "With Clave, it always seems the best strategy for advice is to ask someone else."

Nicholas stared up at the ceiling. "Jeef, any advice?"

Be yourself, Jeef said.

"Any useful advice?" Nicholas asked.

Probably not.

Nicholas decided further discussion wouldn't help.

"Things will work out," Henrietta said.

Nicholas hoped she was right.

That evening, as he was getting ready to teleport to *The Nick of Space,* there was a knock on his door.

He checked the time on his phone. Clave would be waiting for his *I'm ready* message. "I'm busy," he said.

"What are you doing in your room?" his mom asked through the door.

Nicholas felt a wave of warmth flow across his face, and a ripple of guilt grab his stomach. "Nothing."

"You go there every night at exactly the same time," his dad said. "And you've been acting really strange ever since we got back from Australia. What's going on?"

"Nothing."

"Open the door," his mother said.

"I'm not really here," he said as he started to type a message for Clave. "This is a trick."

"Very funny," his dad said. "Open the door right now."

Nicholas put his phone in his pants pocket and crossed the room toward a door he really didn't want to open.

YOUNGEST EMPEROR

It would not be unreasonable to wonder whether Nicholas was the youngest emperor of all time. But "reason" is the construction of sentient beings, and the universe doesn't care what they want or need. It is reasonable only by accident. As for younger emperors, there were many, including Grabinch Memumet of Sligbar XII, who was inaugurated at birth, and fled the position as soon as they were old enough to understand that their duties would interfere with their nap time. While inauguration at the age of zero might seem the youngest, many believe the record was held by Smehn Verd Cophre, whose egg was named emperor two weeks before it hatched, due to a series of miscommunications among the Syndics.

But the average age, either the mean or the median, would be far higher than Nicholas's tender span of a dozen years, given that some emperors have lived for hundreds of years, and at least one, Cyril the Overstayer, just made it past the age of one thousand before he was assassinated by his great-great-great-great-great-great-granddaughter, Debnik the Impatient. To her dismay, she was not chosen by the Syndics to fill the vacancy.

Historians have found no correlation between the age of an emperor and outcome of his reign, unless they were hoping to find one before they started looking. In which case, that's exactly what they found. History is not immune to biases.

BELIEVE IT
OR NOT

"Roach brains," Nicholas muttered, tossing out his favorite expression of dismay quietly enough so it wouldn't be overheard. He opened his door six inches and faced his mom and dad, who both wore that worried expression parents have when they're afraid they're going to have to give their kid a serious lecture about the dangers of some sort of bad or reckless behavior.

While Nicholas's behavior had been unusual, deceptive, and secretive (not counting his recent outburst), it could not in any way be labeled as bad. It could get wildly dangerous, but that was part of the fun, and not something he'd feel guilty about sneaking off-planet to do or concealing from parental units.

Until this moment, he'd felt fairly secure about his

chances of avoiding detection, since his parents generally spent their evenings engrossed in movies from the 1970s, or rehearsing new songs for their act. They seemed oblivious to the fact that they attracted an audience so young that the kids would happily listen to the same song over and over for the entire length of a concert. They almost never showed any interest in whatever happened to their son in his room when the door was closed. Or even when it was open. And he'd resisted the urge to fill his room with some of the amazing alien technology he'd encountered across the universe, like a Thinkerator, a news portal, or a dual-handled tusk buffer. (While he had no tusks in need of buffing, the device sounded like an authentic light saber when set to ULTRA SPEED BUFF, and was a lot of fun to slash around as its seventeen high-speed motors tried to gyroscopically wrestle themselves free of his grip.)

The silence grew until his mother broke it. "Whatever you've been doing, just tell us. We're your parents and we love you."

"We'll understand," his dad said, throwing out an awkward wink of the sort one's eye might make when struck by an unexpected flying insect, or poked with a sharp stick. "Believe it or not, we were kids, once, ourselves."

As Nicholas was trying to fabricate the perfect lie to

cover his nightly seclusion, he realized there was a much better solution. It was so wild and bold, his mind instantly tried to talk itself out of it.

Don't do it!

But he pushed that thought down. The idea felt right. Even more than that, it felt necessary.

He wouldn't make up a story. He'd tell his parents the truth.

He realized he'd been brainwashed by a common trope—though he had no idea this is what it was called. A steady diet of comic books and movies where the superhero struggled to hide his identity from the world had conditioned Nicholas to think in terms of secrecy. Batman and Superman jumped through hoops to conceal their identities. So did nearly all the others. (Except for Hoopman, an obscure hero who died a tragic and horrifying death when he tried to jump through himself.)

Along with being orphaned (which, fortunately, does not play a role in Nicholas's story) and discovering special powers (sorry, nope), secrecy was one of the most common tropes in the superhero genre.

But, really, as he gave the matter serious thought, Nicholas didn't see any reason to hide his title from his parents. This wasn't a comic book or movie. This was his increasingly complex and demanding life. Telling the truth would make things so much simpler in so many ways. As his body relaxed, he saw that the constant vigilance required for keeping secrets, even from his relatively clueless immediate relatives, had filled him with an overdose of stress. Maybe that's why he'd blurted out the truth the other day. Maybe he wanted them to know. And maybe he wanted them to be proud of him.

They'd never have one of those MY SON IS AN HONOR STUDENT bumper stickers. But they could be the only people on Earth, or anywhere else, for that matter, who could slap on a MY SON IS THE EMPEROR sticker. Or MY SON COULD HAVE YOU VAPORIZED.

He glanced down at his shirt pocket, where Henrietta was nestled in preparation for their teleportation to Clave's ship.

"Should I tell them?" he whispered.

While there was no need of quiet conversation at the moment, whispering was another behavior he'd been conditioned to perform, since he usually brought Henrietta to school with him, hidden in a pocket. And especially since that school was a middle school, where any unusual behavior, unpopular opinion, or even the wrong color socks could become ammunition for a social execution. He really didn't want to get mocked for talking to his clothing, and stuck with some dreadful nickname like Shirt-head or Shirt-talker.

Henrietta, who had her forepaws braced on the top edge of the pocket, nodded and, somehow, shrugged. Like most human gestures made by sentient gerbils, it was almost unbearably cute.

"Stop mumbling," his dad said. "Just confess. You'll feel better."

"Okay," Nicholas said. "You know that thing I shouted about in the kitchen?"

"About being emperor?" his mom asked.

His dad frowned and turned to his mom. "I thought he'd said 'vampire.'"

"No, it was emperor," his mom said. "I'm pretty sure that's what he shouted."

"That makes more sense," his dad said. "It was day-time. That would be bad for a vampire. And I don't imag-ine, if there were vampires, the universe would have just one. So, yeah, I guess he said he was emperor."

"What about it?" his mom asked him.

"Well, it's true. I really am the emperor of the universe. I wasn't kidding about that. It's totally true." He couldn't help smiling. This felt even better than the time two years ago when he'd brought home a better-than-usual report card.

Once again, his parents stared at him. Then they stared at each other. Then, they stared back at him. Nicholas wondered whether the Ubiquitous Matrix had suddenly flipped over and now kept people from understanding each other at all.

"You're the emperor of the universe?" his dad asked.

"Yup," Nicholas said. "I sure wasn't expecting it. I just happened to be around at the right time. They needed a new one." Nicholas's smile broadened as he realized how lucky he'd been. A lot of stuff happened to put him at the center of the universe's attention just as the previous emperor was crumbling into dust. Some of it was terrible. Some of it was wonderful. But all of it wove together into the fabric of his current reality.

"Who exactly decided this?" his mom asked.

"The Syndics," Nicholas said. "Well, the people throughout the universe pretty much unanimously proclaimed it. But it was up to the Syndics to make it official."

His dad turned to his mom. "I didn't see anything about this in the newspaper. Did you?"

"Nothing," his mom said. "It wasn't on television, either. Not that the news talks about anything except for gas prices these days."

It sounded like they still didn't believe him. They definitely weren't taking him seriously. He could sort of understand that. He remembered how puzzled he'd felt when he'd first heard that he'd been selected to be emperor. He'd been standing on the bridge of an alien spaceship at the time, after a series of amazing adventures, so it wasn't like he'd been unprepared for surprises. His parents, on the other hand, were totally unaware that the universe was crawling with all manner of life-forms.

He felt that was no excuse for his parents to make jokes about it. They seemed to feel differently.

"It wasn't even in the local paper," his dad said.

"Or the school newsletter," his mom said.

"That's because nobody on Earth knows!" Nicholas shouted. He rushed out more details, hoping to convince them. "When you were away, I got teleported to an alien ship that had abducted Henrietta. I rescued her, and had a pretty major adventure. It started out badly, and a couple planets got destroyed, but it ended up with me becoming the emperor."

There. The truth was out. His relief grew even wider and deeper, washing away the stress from muscles that had been clutching his bones in a shroud of secrecy for far too long. This was great. He wouldn't have to hide anything from his parents ever again—at least, not about being emperor.

He wouldn't have to watch what he said or sneak around. He could fill his room with all sorts of marvelous devices. He could even watch the news from the comfort of his bed. The relief gave him so much pleasure, he contemplated confessing his role in the destruction of the microwave last year, or the couch the year before that, but decided that one revelation at a time was enough. He'd keep those accidents secret for another decade or two.

"Is this an online role-playing thing or something?" his mom asked. "If that's what's going on, it's fine. A little bit of make-believe isn't going to hurt you, even if some of those games do tend to get a bit more violent than I like. A young person needs a good imagination. But you just have to be careful not to lose touch with reality. And be very careful about who you talk to. The internet is full of bad people."

"Maybe he needs to join a baseball league," his dad said to his mom.

"Team sports are good," his mom said.

"No, seriously, listen to me," Nicholas said. "I saved the universe. Actually, Jeef saved it. But Clave, Henrietta, and I helped. Clave's a Menmarian courier and sfumbler. Jeef's a cow. Well, she was a cow before she got fragmented and spread throughout the universe. There was an antimatter power core in a dormant volcano used by the fragmentation cult on the planet Zeng. It created a devouring singularity that reversed the expansion of the universe." He clamped his mouth shut as he realized he was dangerously close to babbling.

"Zeng?" his mom said.

"What a silly comic-book name," his dad said. "You need to make better choices in your reading."

"It's *not* my imagination. It all really happened. And I can prove it. Henrietta can talk." Nicholas lifted her from his pocket and placed her on his shoulder. "Tell them."

Henrietta looked at him and sniffed. His parents looked at him and frowned.

For a billionth of a second, Nicholas felt a wave of doubt. Were his parents right? Had he somehow imagined all of this? Had he dreamed about Zeng, Menmar, Morglob, Spott, and all the other people and places he'd encountered?

No. His adventure was too recent and too real in his mind to be anything but the truth, and too wild to be the product of his own imagination. And his phone never needed to be charged. He pulled it from his pocket and checked for the tiny adapter Clave had installed. It was there, harnessing power from the ether.

Nicholas realized Henrietta was silent because it was her nature to be cautious. He thought about asking Jeef to speak, but he was pretty sure a voice coming from nowhere would be too big a leap for his parents to handle. He'd save her for later. For now, Henrietta would be more than enough to prove he was telling the truth.

"Seriously, tell them," he said. "Go ahead. And then, we can stop hiding. We can install a Thinkerator in my room and get all kinds of cool stuff!"

"I can talk," Henrietta said. "That's not normally the case. Most gerbils can't communicate with people. Most are actually unaware of the possibility of interspecies communication. I was given self-awareness on an alien ship. The Ubiquitous Matrix allows you to understand me."

"The Matrix was blocked on Earth because of the petroleum," Nicholas added. "But I fixed that by having it removed."

"My word!" Mr. Landrew said, spinning toward his wife. "This is wonderful!"

"Amazing!" Mrs. Landrew said, facing her husband. "It's great!"

"Beyond great!" Mr. Landrew said.

Nicholas's relief returned when he saw that they finally believed him. He couldn't blame them for being a bit skeptical at first. It was definitely a huge reality to accept. "I knew it was the right choice," he told Henrietta.

"It appears that way," she said. "Your shoulders are no longer trying to give your ears a high five."

"Was I that stressed?" Nicholas asked her.

"Most of the time," she said.

Nicholas turned his attention back to his parents.

"I thought he never even opened that book," his dad said to his mom.

"That's what I thought, too," his mom said to his dad. "I guess we were wrong."

"What book?" Nicholas asked as the glow of success started to fade. He had no idea what they were talking about.

"Ventriloquism, of course. But you know that," his dad said. "This is fabulous. All those hours you spent up here practicing have really paid off. It almost seemed like the voice really was coming from your pet. Keep practicing. When you get a bit better at it, you can join the act. But you're already making good progress. The tiny little mouse voice was a nice touch. It's almost believable. Maybe just a bit too squeaky. Keep working on it. But try to stay away from so many fancy words. And I'm not sure pretending to be an emperor is the best approach. Kids can't really relate to emperors, and there's really no reason for an emperor to have a mouse. Maybe you could be a lion tamer with a pet mouse? That could be fun."

"Gerbil," Henrietta said.

"Ventriloquism . . . ?" Nicholas vaguely remembered getting some sort of book on the subject, with a really creepy-looking dummy on the cover, flanked by gifts of wool socks and flannel pajamas, during a deeply disappointing Christmas morning when he was nine or ten.

His mom reached out and petted Henrietta. "It's so cute the way you improvised a dummy. But if you want a real one, we'll be happy to pay for it. We want to encourage your hobbies."

"Especially when they involve entertainment," his dad said. "It's in your blood. Ventriloquism is a great choice. It can really make you popular in school."

Nicholas's blood was close to boiling. He pointed at Henrietta's cage. "In just a couple minutes, I'm going to step in there, and send a message to a spaceship that's waiting for my command. And then, I'm going to vanish in a blinding flash of purple light. When I disappear, you'll believe me."

"Magic, too?" his mom asked. "This gets better and better."

"I dabbled in prestidigitation in my youth," his dad

said. "Hey, there's a deck of cards in the kitchen. Come on, Melanie. I'll show you some tricks."

His parents walked away, chatting with enthusiasm about what an asset Nicholas would be for the act, once he got a bit more polished, found a better voice, worked out a less ridiculous character for himself, toned down the vocabulary, and got a more believable dummy.

"I could run after them and keep talking," Henrietta said.

"It's pointless," Nicholas said. He swallowed against a lump that was trying to form in his throat and told himself it didn't matter whether they believed him. "Once they decide something is true, all the proof in the world won't change their minds. I think something happens to your brain when you become an adult. You develop an immunity to anything that goes against your beliefs."

"It appears that way," Henrietta said. "At least, that's what I believe."

POWER TO
THE PEOPLE

Nicholas can be forgiven for assuming that the mere act of placing plans for unlimited free energy on the internet would immediately allow the technology to spread across the planet. If Clave, before becoming the emperor's companion and chronicler, could be considered a pathetically insignificant sfumbler with a relatively minuscule following for his videos (known formally as Short Form Ubiquitous Matrix Blast Loops and conveniently as sfumbles), Nicholas was so far below even that level of notice on all social media platforms he dabbled with as to be deemed nearly nonexistent. Essentially, Nicholas was to the internet as Earth was to the universe.

Random people saw the plans, just as random people

will see anything that gets posted anywhere on the internet, but all the earliest viewers were incapable of understanding those plans. Eventually, six months after Nicholas's original postings were made, an engineering student at a university in Manila with an open mind and poor typing skills stumbled across the plans by accident while trying to look up the best price for car batteries. He easily understood the plans, and made a successful prototype of the device, but failed to get any of his professors to look at it since they knew unlimited free energy was an impossible dream, and even if it were possible it would have been invented by someone with an advanced degree, and not some insignificant student. (In truth, the technology Nicholas tried to share was just as possible as a hydroelectric dam or a wind turbine. It just used a source of power that was unknown on Earth at the time.) Frustrated, the student stayed awake for the next thirty-seven hours, posting the plans everywhere he could think of.

Word spread more quickly after that, and within a year, pretty much everyone on Earth had access to unlimited energy. But all of that happened well after the spectacular end of this story, so let's move on.

ONE FOOT AFTER THE OTHER

I tried to tell my parents I'm emperor," Nicholas said when he reached the control room. "They didn't believe me."

"And they mocked my voice," Henrietta said.

Instead of offering any sort of support or sympathy, Clave said, "The Syndics want to meet with you."

"Why?" Nicholas asked. He hadn't seen them since he'd been crowned, and still wasn't sure what they did, other than wait around to name the next emperor.

"They didn't tell me," Clave said. "Why would they? I'm just a glorified courier."

"And a famous sfumbler," Nicholas said.

"Well, that's true," Clave said. "I definitely have a following. Not as many loyal fans as *Cooking with Fleexbeezle,* yet. But my audience is still growing."

"You made Spott famous," Henrietta said.

"By accident," Clave said.

"And you helped save the universe," Nicholas said. He listed a few other outstanding things about Clave. Then he took a seat and watched as Clave prepared the jump cubes.

"So your parents didn't believe you?" Clave said after the final cube had settled into its compartment.

"Yeah." Nicholas was surprised by the shift in the conversation, and the fact that Clave had actually heard him. "I had Henrietta talk, to help prove my story, and they thought I was learning ventriloquism."

"Why do you care if they believe you or not?" Clave asked.

"If they believe I'm emperor, I can stop hiding everything from them," Nicholas said.

"If they believe you, you can stop hiding?" Clave said. "Did you really just pump those words in the air?"

"Yeah. I did. What's the problem?"

"I'm going to let you think about that for a while," Clave said. He turned toward the navcom and set their course to the jump node.

"What do you mean?" Nicholas asked.

Clave didn't respond.

"What does he mean?" he asked Henrietta.

"Think about it," she said.

"Not you, too." Nicholas looked around the room. "Jeef?" he asked. Given how much she liked explaining things, he was sure she'd offer an explanation.

Jeef replied, but her answer seemed a bit distant, as if she were on the other side of the hatch that led out of the cockpit.

"What was that?" Nicholas asked.

It's better for you to figure it out, yourself, Jeef said.

Having no remaining advisors, and no other choice, Nicholas actually thought about what he'd said. And then, he said aloud the two things he'd thought as he thought it through a second time:

"They didn't believe I'm the emperor.

"If they believe I'm emperor, I can stop hiding that from them.

"Oh," he said as everything clicked into place. "If they don't believe me—if they can't believe me no matter what proof I show, that's just as good as getting them to believe me. Either way, I don't have to hide anything. No matter what they see, they'll come up with some other explanation."

"Barbarians," Clave muttered. But he said it with a smile.

They traveled to Farmengila, the former location of the imperial headquarters until Nicholas had moved it to Earth. Though that change was in name only, since everything related to the emperor had been left in place. While tradition required the headquarters to be at the center of the universe, astrophysics suggested that every place equally qualified for that position, so it was all good.

After the Syndics gave Nicholas their ritual salute, Premblad, the head Syndic, stepped forward and said, "Have you chosen the theme for your reign?"

"The what?" Nicholas asked.

"Theme," Premblad said.

This repetition did nothing to clarify things for Nicholas. As far as he knew, themes were some magical component of novels and short stories that only teachers were capable of seeing. He glanced at Clave, who seemed equally clueless. Then he glanced down at Henrietta.

"No idea," she said.

"Jeef?" Nicholas said, hoping she'd come through for him.

"Jeef?" Premblad asked. "That's your theme? Could you explain?"

"No. Wait." Nicholas scrunched his face. Premblad, who spoke with what any Earth parent would call "an outdoor voice" drowned out whatever reply Jeef had given.

"I'll announce your decision," Premblad said. "Your theme is Jeef. Whatever that is. I'm glad that's settled."

"That's not my theme," Nicholas said. "I need more information. What was the last emperor's theme?"

"His goal was to meet as many of his subjects as possible," Premblad said. "His theme was *Bringing the Emperor to the People.*"

Premblad, along with most of the rest of the universe, was unaware that the previous emperor wanted to meet large groups so he could drain their vitality and live forever.

"Can I think about it?" Nicholas asked.

"Certainly," Premblad said. "But it would be good not to wait too long. You need to think of your legacy."

"Legacy?" Nicholas asked. He searched his modest lexicon for a meaning of that word which would make sense. Nothing came to mind.

"Of course," Premblad said. "It's crucial to make sure your subjects think well of you after you're gone."

"Gone?"

"Gone."

"Like dead gone?"

"Yes. Dead gone," Premblad said. "Unless humans don't die. Though, from what I've seen they're very good at that."

"Yeah. We die. But I don't want to think about my own death," Nicholas said.

But after they returned to the ship, Nicholas was able to think about nothing else.

MISSION
IMPROBABLE

The emperor does not have to define a mission, platform, agenda, or goal. This has not stopped nearly every emperor from doing so. What is the point of being the most powerful entity in the universe without putting that power to use?

Unfortunately, most emperors were also incapable of seeing beyond their own needs, interests, or desires, or those of their own specific type of life-form. Thus, to cite one of the more extreme examples, Emperor Fob the Energetic dedicated his reign to finding the perfect cup of gasbug tea. Given that the gasbugs existed only on Fob's home planet, the search for better ingredients proved futile. On the other hand, it kept the emperor fully occupied for his whole reign, which most historians believe was a good thing.

This is not to imply that no emperors have ever chosen noble goals. There have been attempts to eradicate all diseases, end poverty, and bring equality to places where not all beings were treated equally. Some emperors achieved limited success in their efforts. At least three emperors decided their mission was to end all wars. All three perished in tragic accidents not long after announcing their plans. This was not a coincidence. Nor was it a randomly chosen example, as we will soon see.

YOU'RE HISTORY!

Back in his room, Nicholas stared out his window. He knew that, to everyone else on Earth, the stars were just flickering bits of light. They had no idea about the endless and varied life-forms that orbited those stars. But while the universe was filled with wonders and teeming with life, the sight of the night sky far too often nudged Nicholas's mind to the horrors he'd witnessed.

"There's a lot of violence and pain out there," he said.

"And a lot of beauty," Henrietta said.

"I guess. But a bit of violence can ruin a whole lot of beauty." Nicholas leaned his forehead against the glass, and wondered whether he could make a difference. If he helped end a million wars, there would still be infinite wars. He shared that thought with Henrietta.

"But if you were on one of the planets where a war was stopped, you'd be glad," she said. "Just because you can't save everyone doesn't mean you shouldn't save someone. Right?"

"I guess."

"Think about it from their viewpoint."

"I'm trying." Nicholas imagined someone saving him from a terrible situation. Then, he imagined himself as the savior. The fact that he'd experienced both sides of that relationship during his adventures in space made it easy to appreciate Henrietta's idea. He'd rescued Jeef several times, despite the risks he'd faced by doing it. And Spott had rescued him from certain death. "Maybe that can be my mission. End war. End it throughout the universe."

"That would be wonderful," Henrietta said. "So many lives would be saved. And so much misery would be avoided."

"But I have no idea how to even start," Nicholas said. "How

do you get anyone to realize that there's always a better answer than killing everyone who disagrees with you?"

"Give it time," Henrietta said. "Maybe you'll get an idea."

Nicholas flopped down on his bed. "What about you, Jeef? Any suggestions?"

But he fell asleep before she could even start to think about that.

The next evening, Nicholas grabbed a bag of Doritos before Clave beamed him up. Clave had grown fond of the snack.

"Is there any kind of instruction book for emperors?" Nicholas asked.

"Not that I know of," Clave said through a mouthful of chips.

"Rule book?"

"Nope."

"Guidelines?"

"Nah."

"So there's nothing to tell me how to do a good job," Nicholas said. He grabbed a handful of chips for himself. "You'd think the Syndics would have come up with something. It's not like there's some sort of school for aspiring emperors."

"There are plenty of history books," Clave said.

"Ew . . ." Nicholas said.

"Sorry," Clave said. "Didn't mean to speak with my mouth full. As much as I've studied this place, I have a hard time remembering all the things you barbarians dislike."

"No. It's not that. Though you are pretty disgusting when you eat. It's history," Nicholas said with a shudder. "It's all just a bunch of dates and names."

"Are you kidding?" Clave said, putting down the bag. "History is amazing. *You're* history. *We're* history. The great mapping is history. The battle for Tau Zercese, the Keplefun Project, the Sun Slinger Disaster— all of those are amazing to read about. They're truly exciting. I'll get you some books about great emperors."

Clave activated the Thinkerator and pulled up a catalog of history books.

"Uh, okay . . . thanks." The last thing Nicholas wanted was more assigned reading. But some of the things Clave mentioned did sound interesting. And Nicholas realized he liked reading about the past just fine when he wasn't forced to do it. "Hey, could I eliminate required reading wherever it exists?" he asked.

"Maybe," Clave said. "But how would you enforce that?" He tapped a selection on the catalog that shimmered in the air in front of him. The Thinkerator's jets appeared and a mist descended, coalescing into a thick book.

Nicholas shrugged. "Never mind. But . . . wait! Could I eliminate the position of emperor?"

Clave's eyebrows descended the 1/32nd of an inch that indicated he was frowning. "Why would you do that?"

"Well, it would be sort of cool," Nicholas said. He couldn't help laughing at the absurdity of this. "Really. Think about it. The emperor eliminates himself. Do you see how amazing that would be? It's like totally stupid and awesomely amazing at the same time."

"I agree with the first part of that." Clave ordered a second book. "But if you did that, you'd no longer be emperor."

"And the universe would be different how?" Nicholas asked.

"It would be a poorer place," Clave said.

"In what way?" Nicholas asked.

"I'm not sure. But I know it would." He pointed to the stack of books on the table. "Is that enough to get you started?"

"More than enough," Nicholas said.

They lapsed into silence, then, except for the satisfying crunch of the Doritos.

Ten minutes later, as Clave stared into the depths of an empty bag, he said, "So, you're not going to eliminate yourself. Right?"

"Right," Nicholas said.

Clave wiped his hands on his shirt. "Good decision. Enough of this heavy talk. Let's go somewhere fun."

He wouldn't say anything more about their destination, though his eyebrows did move slightly above their neutral position, indicating he was enthusiastic about what lay ahead.

He took them to a small planet dotted with either large islands or small continents surrounded by green-tinged oceans.

When they landed, they were met by creatures that resembled large bouncy balls of various colors.

"Pick one and hop on," Clave said.

"Seriously?"

"Unseriously, if that's a word," Clave said. "Murkaptins love to give rides."

Nicholas stepped up to the nearest creature and took a seat on top. The surface felt rubbery but firm enough to hold his weight.

"Okay?" he asked.

"Lovely," the creature said. "I'm Tanzi. This will be fun."

"I think I'll stay back here," Henrietta said. "I'd rather not get bounced out of your pocket."

"Good idea." Nicholas put her down and she skittered back up the ramp.

"Hang on," Tanzi said.

Two rings emerged in front of Nicholas. He grabbed hold of them and let out an involuntary squeal of delight at the first bounce. That was followed, on a regular basis, by laughs and cries of delight.

It was a fun ride, with Clave bouncing along next to him and dozens of other Murkaptin leaping and bounding on all sides. Nicholas felt like he was in a high-budget animated film. The Murkaptins gave their visitors a tour of the town.

"Do you ever have wars here?" he asked after they'd headed out of town.

"What are those?"

"Lucky you," Nicholas said. He pushed his quest for a mission out of his mind, as much as he could, and let himself relax.

When they stopped for a break at a river, Nicholas slid off, stretched, and said, "That was a ball."

Tanzi emitted a high-pitched squeal from beneath its

left flipper. A fine purple mist rose from the corners of all six eyelids and filled the air.

The mist smelled like a month-old corpse.

Nicholas turned away from Tanzi and hurled his lunch in an arc over the riverbank. That was followed by his breakfast, and possibly several inches of stomach lining and intestine.

He noticed Clave standing calmly in place, watching him.

"What just happened?" Nicholas asked after he'd wiped his mouth on his sleeve.

"You made him laugh," Clave said. "That's never a good idea. I guess I should have warned you."

"I wasn't trying to be funny," Nicholas said. He looked down at his splattered shirt, and promised himself he'd try to do a better job chewing his food from now on.

"I guess you just have a gift," Clave said. "They love bad puns."

Nicholas brushed a few of the larger chunks from his shirt. "That's how they laugh?"

"Yes. That's how they laugh."

"It's awful," Nicholas said.

"You should see how they cry," Clave said.

"I'd rather not." He realized he'd been the only one to react to the odor. "Hey, why didn't it bother you?"

Clave grabbed the sides of his nostrils and pulled something from his nose. "Plugs," he said. "Everyone knows to use them when talking with a Murkaptin."

"I didn't," Nicholas said. "You should have warned me."

"I guess I should." Clave held out the plugs, which glistened with a fine coating of slimy secretions. "Want them?"

"No!" Nicholas backed away. "It's not like I'll throw up again."

Halfway along the ride back to the ship, he discovered he was wrong about that when he accidentally issued another bad pun. But he managed to avoid falling off the Tanzi as he hurled the remaining contents of his stomach across the landscape. He filed that away in the list of his few athletic achievements, along with a promise that he would try his best never to visit this planet again.

IMPOLITE SOCIETIES

Virtually every widely discussed conspiracy theory is pretty much untrue. The more popular a belief, the less likely it is accurate. This does not mean there are no secret societies who profit from the control, exploitation, and misery of others. It means the most successful and dangerous clandestine groups have done a highly successful job of making sure the "secret" aspect of their secret society was rigidly protected.

The Unilluminated—who'd named themselves that because they kept their workings secret by constructing a heavily cloaked base of operations—were among the few groups aware that Nicholas's predecessor, Emperor Zil, was capable of endless rejuvenation. That was fine with them. They had put him in power in the first place, and had enjoyed the benefits of his long reign. The effort to force the selection of a candidate who suited their goals was large enough that longevity was a major positive factor in their choice. His death caught them unprepared, as did Nicholas's coronation. They met immediately, to decide whether he would conflict with their vast program of exploiting both those who desired to purchase devastating weapons of destruction and their highly successful tactic of mining the wealth from planets so ravaged by war that there was nobody left to stop them. It should be noted that the planet torcher, a horrendous weapon that had left such an indelible scar on Nicholas's memory, was one of their finest and most profitable creations.

Urbanis, the current leader, opened the meeting without any preamble. "He's young. Inexperienced. He could be molded to our needs."

"Or eliminated," Solanis said. "That would be easier. We have several suitable candidates to replace him. If we'd had any warning Zil would die, or if the Syndics hadn't acted so quickly to fill the vacancy, we wouldn't even have this problem."

The others nodded. Except for one.

"If he falls in line, retaining him would be easier still," Teritus said. "He has already carved a marvelous path of destruction in a short period of time. We've seen the reports. He seems to have a gift for creating instability."

"He does," Solanis said. "Though he also brought peace to a major conflict."

"It could go either way," Teritus said. "But he is young. And the young of most sentient life-forms do enjoy the thrill of mindless destruction. If he's properly guided, he will serve us well."

"We'll wait," Urbanis said. "But if he shows signs of being a peacekeeper, we will eliminate him. We need to be prepared for that." He looked toward Teritus.

"I will arrange for his execution if the need arises." Teritus stood. "If you will excuse me, I need to set things in motion immediately. He's already heading back to his home planet."

SODA SPEAK

Two more weeks of school had gone by since Nicholas's return to the classroom. "Three weeks left," he said as he took his seat in algebra. That was good—he wasn't all that much of a fan of school. But it was also bad, because once summer vacation started he wouldn't get to be in the same room with Stella five days out of each week.

They'd talked a bit, at times, as they moved between classes. But there hadn't been anything approaching a real conversation. Not that he hadn't been offered ample opportunities. She'd reached into his pocket more than once to give Henrietta a fond skritch on the head. Each time she approached him, he'd thought about asking her on a date. But he wasn't exactly sure how all of that worked.

The bell rang. Nicholas got up and headed for the hall.

"Hey," Stella said, walking up next to him. "Want to grab a Coke or something after school?"

"Uh, YEAH!!!" Nicholas said. He tried to gulp back at least two of the three exclamation points he'd spewed into the air. "I mean, um, sure. That would be okay."

"Problem solved," Henrietta said as Nicholas turned off toward his next class.

"Or redirected," Nicholas said. His brain spun into overdrive as he tried to get mentally prepared for something far more mysterious than any planet he'd ever visited.

They had English class together last period. The teacher, Ms. Revner, greeted them with a smile. "Wonderful news, class. The department has been working with social studies, and we've decided that you'll be doing a joint-discipline paper for the two classes."

The reaction of the students seemed to suggest that they had different criteria for the application of *wonderful* to any particular piece of news.

Ms. Revner went on to outline the grim requirements

of the assignment, drawing increasing groans from her audience despite repeatedly signaling for them to be quiet.

Great, Nicholas thought. *I have to rule the universe, solve endless problems, take out the garbage, and write a paper.*

Ms. Revner, who refused to use the student messaging system for assignments, passed out copies of a single sheet of paper. "This lists some typical topics you might consider for your theme."

"Theme!" Nicholas said.

Heads turned.

Nicholas ducked his own head down. He'd totally forgotten his promise to the Syndics that he'd find a theme for his reign, probably because the one idea he'd come up with, finding a way to end all wars, seemed impossible.

"Remind me to look at the list," he whispered to Henrietta as he left the class.

But he put all of that aside as he walked with Stella to Grab a Slab, a chain burger place that had just opened a new location in town. They got pops—root beer for Nicholas, grape for Stella—then took seats opposite each other in a booth. They locked eyes. They unlocked eyes. They locked eyes again.

I have no idea what to say, Nicholas thought.

He dropped his napkin, then bent over to grab it. As Henrietta clutched his chest with her needle-like claws, he whispered, "Jeef, what should we talk about?"

Jeef replied in a whisper, but Nicholas couldn't make out what she said.

"Are you all right?" Stella asked.

"Yeah . . . Ow!" Nicholas bumped his head on the edge of the table. "Dropped my napkin . . ."

They repeated the meeting and fleeing of eyes.

I've traveled the universe, Nicholas reminded himself. But he didn't think that would be a good thing to mention on a first date. Or a hundredth. Not without sounding like exactly the sort of fantasy-addled kid his parents accused him of being.

No, he couldn't tell her where he'd traveled. But he knew the perfect question to ask her.

"If you could go anywhere, where would you go?"

"Paris," Stella said. She took a sip of her drink.

The answer nearly derailed him. He'd been thinking on a larger scale. "Paris is nice. But what if you could go anywhere in the entire universe? The sky's the limit. No. That's wrong. There is no limit. If you could go absolutely anywhere in the entire universe, where would you go?"

"Saturn," Stella answered almost as quickly as she'd picked Paris.

"Saturn?" Nicholas asked.

"Saturn," Stella repeated. "Sure. Think how amazing that would be."

"But that's like just going down the street to your favorite store when you could go to somewhere far off and awesome like Ethiopia or Singapore," Nicholas said.

"You didn't say it had to be far away," she said. "You asked me where I wanted to go. And that's my answer. The fact that it's close isn't meaningful. If my favorite store was right down the street from my house, I wouldn't go somewhere else just because it was farther away."

Nicholas tried to wrap his mind around Saturn's place in the many wonders he'd seen. He'd been to a planet made of molten iron, and another where the trees sang and the birds left colored trails in the air as they flew. Saturn was just a big glob of gas. True, it had amazing rings. But so did a lot of planets. And once you saw the rings, there really wasn't much more you could do except scan the banded atmosphere in search of interesting patterns. Saturn was an inhospitable out-the-window marvel, not a let's-land-and-have-an-adventure destination like Spott's home planet of Beradaxia with its deep canyons and towering waterfalls. It would be beyond awesome to take Stella there. But there was no way that could happen. He couldn't even tell her about it.

"Yeah, Saturn is cool," he said. He realized he didn't sound all that convincing. He tried to think of something else to say about it, but nothing came to mind, so he decided to drop the topic of intergalactic tourism and move to the more comfortable subject of which of their teachers were the best—aside from the obvious choice of Ms. Galendrea—and which should find another career cutting down forests or neutering cattle.

But on the way home from Grab a Slab, he imagined what it would be like to take Stella for a ride past Saturn. And, knowing how Clave tended to navigate, he was fairly certain that at some point there'd be a lurch, a jolt, or unexpected deceleration, and he'd save Stella from harm as they tumbled toward the bulkhead.

"Why are you breathing so rapidly?" Henrietta asked, breaking into Nicholas's fantasies.

"Walking too quickly, I guess," he said.

"You were standing still, staring at the clouds," she said. "I could hear your heart beating."

"I was thinking about walking fast," he said. "It's the same thing."

He resumed walking. And thinking. But he was very glad Spott wasn't there to read his mind.

ARG!

The night after his rescue, Morglob paid a visit to the captain of the pirate ship. He'd waited outside the cabin until he heard loud uninterrupted snores of a beast deeply asleep. Then he oozed beneath the door and made his way to the captain's hammock. The climb up the wall was difficult, but Morglob was determined. From there, he was able to flow over the captain's face, stopping both the snores and the spark of life in the scurvy pirate.

"Captain Morglob," he said, testing out his new title. A ripple crossed his surface. This was the Phleghmhackian equivalent of a negative head shake. That title didn't suit him. He was far grander than any pirate. Grander than a captain or even an admiral. He was a mogul, at the very least. A mover and shaker. Better yet, he was a titan of the entertainment industry. Or, at least, he'd been one on the day he'd been launched into space.

While he had exploited hundreds of talented actors, singers, dancers, and comedians throughout his decades as the most powerful talent agent in the universe, this was his first murder. He paused to appreciate the surge of power that came from it. Then, he dripped off the corpse and switched on the news, presented by a perfect being who looked exactly like him, down to the tiniest quivering detail.

I love me so much, he thought.

He was hoping the top story would be about his absence. It wasn't. It was about the new emperor, and some stupid visit he'd made to some stupid planet to solve some stupidly unimportant and easily solved problem. Morglob didn't pay too much attention to it.

The second story was also about the emperor, following up on a planet he'd visit the other day. A close-up of the emperor caught Morglob's attention.

Before the end of the third story, Morglob's murder-fueled sense of accomplishment turned to rage, and his thoughts turned to revenge.

A SOCK TO
THE FACE

Y ou seem exceedingly cheerful this evening," Clave
said when Nicholas stepped onto the bridge. He
switched on his sfumbler. "Anything your fans and my
followers might be interested in?"

Nicholas was going to issue a denial, but he realized
he didn't have to hide anything from Clave—but not
for the same reason he didn't have to hide things from
his parents. The Menmarian would mock him no matter what he said. Whether he told the truth or invented
a reason for his mood, Clave would make fun of him.
It would be affectionate mocking, but it would still be
mocking. So he told the truth. "I had a nice talk with a
girl. And we went for a pop."

Clave switched off the sfumbler and made a face. "That's disgusting."

"What? No way. Girls are awesome," Nicholas said. "Especially this one. But if you like guys, that's cool. My uncle has a boyfriend."

"I wasn't talking about her," Clave said. "I meant the beverage. I don't understand your fondness for carbonated liquids supersaturated with sugars. It's a perfect way to ruin a perfectly good glass of water."

"I wouldn't expect you to understand it," Nicholas said. "Let's check out the headlines." He always looked forward to watching Stella Astrallis give the top stories of the day.

"Maybe we can skip it for a change," Clave said. "We really need to get to Hagion VI. They're trying to end a war involving themselves and three other planets."

"It won't take long," Nicholas said. "A couple of minutes won't make a difference." As much as it felt great to try to stop a war, the joy was brief in the face of reality. It seemed like six others would pop up for each one he helped quell. Sometimes, that would even happen on the same planet he'd just helped. Stopping them one at a time wasn't good enough. He needed to figure out how bring about a universal peace.

"But we really—"

"News flash," Nicholas said, triggering Stella and interrupting Clave.

The first story was about his recent visit to Perlak. Nicholas felt it was important to watch the stories about himself, because he'd learned that there was more than one way to interpret anything he did. The news allowed him to try to do the right thing.

After the top story, Stella presented the usual rundown of wars, disasters, and celebrity news, including a touching tribute to the missing-and-presumed dead super-agent, Morglob Sputum.

The mere mention of that name caused Nicholas, Henrietta, and Clave to shudder.

"I'm glad he's gone," Nicholas said.

"We all are," Henrietta said.

"I wish I'd let him make me a star before we booted him into space," Clave said.

"He didn't seem all that interested in doing that," Nicholas said.

"That was a negotiating tactic," Clave said. "I could tell he was interested. He was playing hard to get so I'd leap at his first offer."

Nicholas decided there was no reason to step on Clave's fantasy. He was much more interested in the news.

"And here's a special note for collectors," Stella said as

she wrapped up the top stories. "With only three hours left before the sale closes, enthusiasm is swelling rapidly among bidders for this unique item at Universal Collectible Auctions Unlimited."

An image appeared next to her of a pair of socks. They looked familiar to Nicholas. As the image zoomed closer, Stella resumed talking.

"This is a pair of socks owned and worn by Emperor Nicholas Landrew."

She said more, but for once in his life, Nicholas turned his attention away from Stella.

"You sold my socks!" Nicholas asked.

"Technically, no. I didn't sell them. I put them up for auction. The auction house will sell them."

"How could you do this?" Nicholas asked. "And why?"

"You're popular," Clave said.

"But you stole my socks," Nicholas said.

"Let's be fair. I traded them for a nice pair made from wool spun from the armpit hairs of Riverbean butter chimps. They're the most comfortable and luxurious socks in the universe. And they do an excellent job of trapping odor."

Nicholas thought back to when Clave had asked for

the socks. "And you made up a ridiculous lie about some aliens hating foot odor."

"I did *not* lie!" Clave said. "I would never lie to you. I looked very hard for a race that would object to the odor of stale human socks or unwashed human feet. Do you have any idea what a difficult search that was? I worked really hard to be truthful. I am *not* a liar!"

"But . . ." Nicholas tried to find words to express his outrage. "You should have asked me."

"And you'd have told me to go ahead?" Clave asked. He pitched his voice in a halfway decent imitation of Nicholas's prepubescent whine. "*Sure, Clave. You can have my socks to auction off. You can have anything you want.* And you would have been fine with that?"

"Absolutely not," Nicholas screamed.

"See? There would have been no point in asking. This way, you're happy, I'm happy, and some lucky highest bidder is extremely happy."

Nicholas could see there was no way he could get Clave to understand how he felt. "Don't ever do this again," he said.

"Of course not," Clave said. "They are guaranteed to be the only pair offered. That's what makes them rare and highly valuable."

"Not just socks," Nicholas said. "None of my clothing. Okay?"

"Okay," Clave said. "So this would be a bad time to suggest you change your shirt?"

"No!" Nicholas screamed. "I mean yes. It would be a terrible time."

"I was kidding," Clave said.

"Let's get going," Nicholas said.

"Yes, Emperor," Clave said, with as much of a smirk as a Menmarian face could muster.

Before he left the ship and headed back home, Nicholas checked the news to see the results of the auction. According to Stella, a bidder who wished to remain anonymous had paid five million dollars for the socks.

"And you get all that money?" Nicholas asked.

"Hardly," Clave said. "The auction house gets a commission. And there are taxes. After expenses, I'll be lucky to get anything at all."

Now, more than ever, Nicholas wished there was an easy way to tell when a Menmarian was lying.

"I thought the emperor had infinite funds," Nicholas said. "Doesn't each planet contribute a dollar a year? And aren't there infinite planets?"

"Yup," Clave said. "But guess how long it takes for all of that money to arrive?"

"An infinite length of time?" Nicholas guessed. He had a sinking feeling in his gut that he was right.

Clave confirmed that guess with a nod.

It seemed unfair to Nicholas that something as incomprehensible as the infinite was constantly messing around in so many ways with the life of one insignificant and totally finite being. "But there should still be a lot of money," he said. He stepped over to the teleporter cage. "Can't you just get whatever you need without doing sketchy things like tricking me out of my socks?"

"You're right. There's a lot coming in," Clave said. "But there are a lot of expenses. The Syndics are not exactly frugal. And there's a whole palace to run. There's really nothing much to spare. And there are ridiculously long forms to fill out for any expenses. The Syndics love paperwork. See you tomorrow."

Clave pressed the button, teleporting Nicholas and Henrietta back to Nicholas's room.

"Do you believe him?" Nicholas asked Henrietta when he stepped out of the cage.

"He's strange, and totally egotistical," she said, "and he doesn't always seem all that well connected with reality, but I never got the feeling he was dishonest. Sneaky, yes. Scheming, sure. Egotistical, absolutely. But dishonest? Not Clave."

"That's good enough for me," Nicholas said. "But I wish I'd known what he was doing."

The moment he spoke those words, Nicholas realized there was someone who should have been able to warn him what was going on.

Nicholas looked up at the ceiling. "Jeef, why didn't you tell me what Clave was doing when he asked for my socks?" He kept his voice low, so his parents wouldn't hear him. Though he realized that if they did, they'd just assume he was practicing ventriloquism.

I wasn't aware he was tricking you, Jeef whispered back.

"But aren't you everywhere, now?" Nicholas asked.

Yes. I'm all places and can know most things. Though some regions are cloaked in ways I don't yet understand. But, as far as I can tell, to perceive everything at all times is beyond my capability. To know is not the same as to perceive. Anything and everything are vastly different quantities.

Nicholas tried to process those words. He failed. "What does that mean?"

Do you feel your shirt? Jeef asked.

"No," Nicholas said. Then he shifted his attention to his arms and chest. And to the space between his collarbones, where the shirt's collar crossed his throat. He could even feel the label where its edge brushed the

back of his neck. "Wait. Well, now I do. After you mentioned it."

*Every inch of your skin can feel things, but you aren't
constantly aware of that,* Jeef said. *Your brain would be
overloaded if it were aware of everything your body could
sense. I'm everywhere. But I still need to focus on* somewhere. *Or, at most, a number of somewheres. I can't absorb everywhere.*

"I think I get it," Nicholas said.

I sense sadness, Jeef said.

"Well, I like it when you're around," he said.

I'm always around, Jeef said. *It's just that there will be
times when I'm not paying attention to you.*

"So you're sort of like a parent," Nicholas said.

Sort of . . .

"Or any adult, for that matter," he added.

Basically . . .

"So what are you doing when you're not paying attention to me?" Nicholas asked.

Searching for my purpose, Jeef said. *Trying to make
sense of my existence.*

"Join the club," Nicholas said.

As he was getting ready for bed, Nicholas noticed a
sheet of paper in his pants pocket. "Might as well look
at it," he said. He skimmed the list of sample themes

his teacher had given the class. When he reached the bottom, he tossed the list onto the pile of papers on his desk. An instant later, as something clicked in his head, he snatched the list from where it had landed. His eyes shot back to the third entry:

What is the meaning of life?

He thought about all the lives that had been snuffed out by pointless wars, and his desire to end war. Maybe, if everyone cared about every life . . . ?

"That's it!" Nicholas shouted.

Henrietta gave him a quizzical look from her cage.

Nicholas crossed the room and squatted down next to her. "What does everyone in the universe have in common?"

Henrietta stared at him and blinked. Obviously, she wasn't going to even take a stab at answering that one.

"They're all alive. Everyone in the universe is alive. So, what does that mean? What is the meaning of life? That's the first part of my quest. I'm going to find the meaning of life."

"First part?" Henrietta asked. "I'm afraid to hear where this is going."

"That's how we end wars," Nicholas said. "If everyone knew for sure that every life had a meaning, maybe they wouldn't be so quick to end other lives."

"Maybe," Henrietta said. "And maybe not."

"It's still better to at least try something. I can't just give up and let countless people die." Nicholas sat back down and allowed himself to try to absorb the mission he had just handed himself.

Be careful what you look for, Jeef said, interrupting Nicholas's thoughts. *You might find it.*

"Huh?" Nicholas asked.

Old saying, "Be careful what you wish for." I was just tweaking it a bit. Like before, she'd whispered her words.

"Hold on," Nicholas said. "Do you already know the answer?"

No, Jeef said.

"Swear," Nicholas asked. He was used to Jeef being a source of wisdom.

I swear, Jeef said.

"Cross your heart?" Nicholas asked.

That would be difficult, Jeef said.

"Sorry. Sometimes, I forget." Nicholas thought back to their first encounter, where Jeef was already reduced from an intact, living cow to a nicely wrapped package of ground beef.

That's okay. I still love you.

"But you promise I'm not going to spend ten years

searching for something and then, at the end of all of this, find out you had the answer all along?"

I promise. I do not have the answer.

"So that's going to be the key to my rule," Nicholas said. "I'll find the meaning of life, and put an end to all wars. Wait . . . You don't know the meaning of life, do you, Henrietta?"

"Definitely not," she said. "Until recently, I didn't even know that was a question."

"Will you at least think about it?" he asked.

"Sure. But maybe not until morning." She burrowed under her cedar shavings.

"Fair enough," Nicholas said. It felt good to have a purpose, even if he had no idea where this quest would lead him. Before he went to sleep, he sent Clave a message.

Tomorrow, take me to visit the wisest being in the universe.

PLANET CAREFULLY

One of the many quaint genres of human literature is called *science fiction*. (Literature, itself, is a fairly quaint concept throughout the universe. Civilizations tend to move away from any form of entertainment that requires thought or effort on the part of the recipient, such as reading, and devour that which they can absorb without effort, such as sfumbles. Though, as anyone who has been paying attention already knows, even the most quaint and rare items are abundant in an infinite universe. But let us get back to that particular genre, for there is a point to all of this.) Every genre has its rules and guidelines. Some of these rules are fairly strict. Science fiction should involve science. (Unless it doesn't.) And some of these rules are fairly fluid. Science fiction should not violate the known rules of physics. (Unless it does.)

One set of these rules for science fiction writers can be found in the groundbreaking writer's guide called *One Set of Rules for Science Fiction Writers,* by the award-winning writer Conner Alexander Fooshwhistle. Again, there are strict rules and lax ones. But the one that currently concerns us is rule #917: There are no planets or civilizations dedicated solely to one trade or craft.

This rule, of course, makes sense when created by and shared with a planet-bound population, such as that of Earth. On a larger scale, it is obviously hogwash. (A word mostly used by those who have never experienced the pleasure of washing a Ferdorian cuddle hog.) Take, for instance, Lebrov XXIV. This is a planet where every resident does nothing but make bottles. Or, more accurately, it *was* such a planet, until the market for Lebrovian bottles vanished and all the Lebrovians starved to death. (Nobody claimed having an entire population do one task was a smart idea. Or even, long term, a viable one.)

And the earliest Thinkerator center eventually occupied most of its planet, and provided occupations for most residents.

So, when Nicholas asked Clave to seek out the greatest philosophers in the universe, Clave had numerous choices of individual thinkers, institutions dedicated to thought, towns thus aligned, as well as cities, countries, continents, and entire planets. There was even a solar system where all the inhabited planets did nothing but ponder the mysteries of the universe. Unfortunately, they were so wrapped up in thought, they never noticed that their sun was dying until it was too late. Ironically, their last moments were also their brightest.

But the removal of that one solar system still left countless other choices in the hands of someone who was not an enthusiastic researcher. After an intense ten or fifteen minutes of effort, which was pretty much Clave's limit when it came to such tasks, he'd narrowed the options down to a manageable number, which he planned to offer to Nicholas. The emperor could make the final decision of which planets to visit before he got tired of the whole silly exercise.

HUH?

I found thirty-eight beings that might be the smartest in the universe," Clave said. He tapped his palm and projected a list in the air. "Each resides on a planet known for dedication to ideas and thoughts."

"Wow, that's a lot," Nicholas said.

Clave highlighted the bottom half of the list, deleted it, and said, "I found nineteen beings that might be the smartest in the universe. Still too many?"

"I don't know. I'll never get my paper done in time if we just visit one a day. Do we have time to visit a bunch?" Nicholas asked.

"We can probably fit in three or four of them, if you don't waste a lot of time asking simple-minded barbarian questions," Clave said.

"I'll do my best," Nicholas said.

They docked above the first planet on the list, Fresvox XIII, and took a shuttle to the surface. From there, local students of the smartest man took Nicholas to meet him. They spanned a variety of species, though Nicholas noticed they all had at least two arms and two legs.

He was led to a room that looked like a small gymnasium.

Nicholas had faced a staggering variety of life-forms since he'd been sucked into space, but he'd never been faced back by five pairs of eyes from a single biped. Yesper's central head was ringed by four smaller ones, evenly spaced around his neck. The one in the rear had tilted to the side and turned, owl-like, one hundred eighty degrees, so it could peer over a shoulder. All five of the mouths were smiling, which did not help in any way to dissipate the air of weirdness.

"Hi," Nicholas said. He was tempted to add, "You all," but decided to leave the greeting as it was.

Instead of responding, Yesper grabbed two dueling swords from a rack on the wall. He tossed one to Nicholas, who actually managed to catch it.

"What's this for?" Nicholas asked.

"We must duel while we talk," Yesper said. "It keeps the mind sharp."

"I hope that's the only sharp thing." Nicholas brushed the tip of his sword with his thumb. Fortunately it seemed dull.

Yesper dropped into a fencing stance. Nicholas mirrored him. Swords clashed.

"Ask your question," Yesper said.

"What is the meaning of life?"

"Die!" Yesper screamed, thrusting his sword against Nicholas's chest. The point didn't break his skin, but the jab stung in a way that reminded Nicholas why he disliked playing catch with a football.

Henrietta skittered out of his pocket and dashed to a corner of the room. "I'll wait here," she said.

"Ouch," Nicholas said. He glanced toward the corner and added, "Good idea."

"Sorry," Yesper said. "I get enthusiastic. So, you want to know the meaning of life. Correct?"

"Correct." Nicholas parried the next jab with a clumsy swipe and tried to score a point. Fencing actually seemed like it might be fun, if they removed the part where mistakes hurt so much.

"What do you mean by *meaning*?" Yesper asked as he gracefully evaded Nicholas's awkward attempt to skewer him.

"What do you mean what do I mean?" Nicholas said.

He paused and thought about the words that had just passed out of his mouth. He wasn't even sure that was what he'd meant to say.

Instead of answering, Yesper added, "And what do you mean by *life?*"

"That's what I'm trying to find out." Nicholas wondered whether Yesper was playing some sort of game. "I mean, we all know what life is. I think . . ."

Yesper jabbed Nicholas in the left shoulder, and then in the right. "You haven't even begun to think. If you are searching for the meaning of something, what exactly are you looking for? What are you hoping to find?"

"I . . ." Nicholas's mouth remained open as he tried to offer an answer and avoid further jabs.

"Shut that gaping mouth. It makes you look stupid." Yesper tapped Nicholas on the cheek with the side of the sword. "You could be looking for the *why* in all of this. Why are we here?"

Nicholas rubbed his cheek with his free hand and started to nod, but Yesper wasn't finished. "Or you could be looking for a purpose," he said, tapping Nicholas on the other cheek.

Another nod got cut short by another addition to the lecture.

"But that could mean *your* purpose, or it could mean the purpose of a creator," Yesper said. "Right?"

"Couldn't those be the same?" Nicholas asked.

"That's actually a glimmer of a spark of a tiny sign of brilliance," Yesper said, lifting his sword in a brief salute.

"Thanks, I think . . ." Nicholas said.

"It's also possible the answer lies beyond us," Yesper said. "It could be beyond our comprehension. Or it could be beyond our reach."

Nicholas paused to absorb this. Until now, he hadn't even considered the possibility that the answer could be out of his reach, or even beyond his ability to understand it. But he hoped that wouldn't be the case. It seemed hugely unfair there was even a possibility life was meaningless or that the meaning itself was incomprehensible.

"The answer could be simple," he said.

"That doesn't matter," Yesper said. "Simplicity isn't the issue. Let's say I pile three stones on the ground, intending them to represent peace, love, and happiness. That's simple enough. And then, let's say I go away. If you see those stones, you might try to guess what they meant. But if we never cross paths, the answer is beyond you."

"That doesn't mean I can't find the right answer," Nicholas said.

"No. The problem is insurmountable," Yesper said as he laid a stinging slash across Nicholas's right side. "Whatever answer you find, even if it happens to be correct, you have no way to know that it's actually the right one. It's not like a math problem, where you can check your solution. Search all you want. You might as well save yourself a lot of time and effort and just make something up."

"No," Nicholas said. "I'm going to find the answer. And when I find it, I'll know it's right."

"Good luck with that," Yesper said, hitting Nicholas directly above the heart with a thrust that was definitely going to leave a bruise. "Your efforts are pointless. As is any further discussion."

"Thanks for talking with me," Nicholas said. He put down the sword, retrieved Henrietta, and headed to the shuttle with Clave, who'd waited for him outside the fencing room.

"Did you get your answer?" Clave asked.

"I don't think so," Nicholas said, rubbing his chest. "What do you think, Henrietta?"

"I think I need to take a break from thinking," she said.

"Lucky you," Nicholas said. He turned back to Clave. "This next place on the list, they don't use a lot of knives or clubs or anything, do they?"

"They are a very civilized race," Clave said. "Of course they use knives, clubs, and guns. But I don't think the person you're seeing will try to hurt you."

"That's a relief," Nicholas said.

This turned out to be true, assuming the act of being bored to death, or drowned underneath an avalanche of word salad, wasn't considered harmful. The remaining visits that day were no less perplexing than Nicholas's encounter with Yesper, but far less painful. By the time he went to bed, his head was buzzing with dozens of thoughts that seemed to have taken up battle with each other.

"Jeef, are you sure you don't have an answer I can use?" Nicholas asked after he'd turned out his light.

I don't.

Nicholas was barely able to hear the words.

"Are you getting quieter, or is it my imagination?"

I'm afraid it's not your imagination, she said.

"Why?" Nicholas asked.

I'm still dispersing. I'm everywhere. But everywhere is expanding. And I'm finite. I guess I can only be stretched so thin.

Nicholas tried to picture this. He failed. But he was

more concerned with the immediate consequences. "Will you fade away?"

I don't know.

"How will we talk?"

Again, I don't know. But I'm searching for answers.

"But what if you don't figure anything out?"

I will, she said. *Now get some sleep. You're wearing yourself out.*

He slept, though he feared she'd be gone when he woke. He couldn't imagine a world, or a universe, without Jeef. They'd been through so much from the time she'd first gained sentience to the time she reassured him that she would help him rule wisely as emperor.

His fear proved true. He called out to her when he woke, but she did not respond.

He tried again. He waited. He listened with all his heart.

"Can you hear her?" he asked Henrietta, hoping her more acute senses would allow him to have another conversation with Jeef, even if it had to be relayed.

"No," Henrietta said. "I can't."

"What do we do now?" he asked Henrietta.

"We carry on with your quest," she said. "That's all we can do. And trust Jeef to find a solution. She'll return."

"I hope you're right," Nicholas said.

He carried on. But the search for the meaning of life seemed destined to fail. After a series of hectic evenings, he'd pretty much given up learning anything he could use for his paper. Or, sadly, anything that could help convince people not to wage wars. "Is there any point going to the last one?" he asked Henrietta.

"Well, it's a good habit to finish what you start," she said.

"What if you start eating a piece of fruit, and it's rotten?" Nicholas asked.

"I guess that would be an exception," Henrietta said. "Let's just go through with it, and see if you learn anything. What's the worst that could happen?"

Unfortunately, the answer to that was far worse than either Nicholas or Henrietta could have guessed.

THE UNIVERSAL QUESTION

Nicholas was obviously far from the first sentient being to search for the meaning of life. Countless individuals have made that search, either in idle moments of thought or through prolonged and intense studies. Endless groups, large and small, have made that their mission. There are entire societies that have felt they found the answer. Some of them lived quite happily with this knowledge, even when outside observers could see the solution they'd selected was a delusion.

While such investigations can be harmless, or even beneficial for those involved, the situation gets more complicated when others are affected by the conclusions. One small group of Denwaldori, for example, believed the meaning of life was to eradicate all life in the universe. They actually managed to create a self-propagating death ray that, once constructed and activated, would have done just that. (Though some historians who have studied this group and the fragmentary remains of the plans for this technology believe it would not have harmed rhinovirus, cockroaches, or celebrity chefs.) Fortunately for life throughout the universe, the Denwaldori grew impatient with the slow development of the final ray, and started ending all life in the universe, beginning with themselves, using existing weapons. It needn't be added that their amazing technological ability was balanced by a stunning lack of common sense.

There are numerous other examples. Ironically, countless lives have been lost by those refusing to accept a specific meaning of life that was being forced on them by others.

ASSASSIN

This one might be a bit weird," Clave said as he brought the ship down to the surface of Ecksel II, a small arid planet in an obscure corner of a galaxy far enough from Earth that its light had not yet spanned the distance.

"Weird how?" Nicholas asked.

"You'll see," Clave said.

"No docking station?" Nicholas asked.

"Too small a population," Clave said. "There are only thirty residents."

"Thirty?"

Clave nodded. The ship tilted, but then he righted it. Nicholas reminded himself not to distract Clave too much during the more critical parts of any piloting sequence.

"Or fifteen," Clave added. "Depending on how you count them."

Nicholas didn't ask for an explanation. "Want to come?" he asked Henrietta when they'd touched down.

"I'll stay here," she said. "I still have half the morning paper to shred."

When Nicholas stepped out of the ship, he was met by a creature that looked like a cartoon version of a lovable beaver. It had huge eyes, buck teeth, and a large, flat tail. It stood on two legs.

"Welcome, Emperor Nicholas," it said. "I represent Senbler."

Nicholas tried to determine the depth of its intelligence from the voice, but that voice itself was a goofy cartoonish chirp pitched higher than he expected.

"Thanks." He didn't ask who or what Senbler was.

"We received your question, and are eager to discuss our answer," the creature said. It turned and waddled toward a grove of trees.

Nicholas followed it through the grove to a clearing. More of the creatures had gathered there. A quick count told Nicholas there were fifteen of them. But Clave had mentioned thirty. He wondered where the rest were.

"So, you know the meaning of life?" he asked.

"We have an answer," all the creatures replied in unison.

That startled Nicholas, but not as much as the explosion that followed, turning the closest creature into a spray of wet protein.

It was no longer cute.

"Aaahhhg!" Nicholas shouted, leaping back.

Someone burst into the clearing, brandishing a weapon that resembled an enormous Super Soaker. But it wasn't pumping water. It was pumping violent disruption of the forces that held matter together.

The killer skidded to a halt just a few feet to Nicholas's left. He swept his weapon in a wide arc, destroying every creature in the grove.

Nicholas reached out to grab the weapon, but the shooter leaped back.

Their eyes met.

The universe lurched in ways that made teleportation seem like a hop and a skip.

Nicholas stared at himself.

His self stared back briefly, then spun away and ran from the clearing, as if Nicholas held no interest for him.

Nicholas staggered as his mind tried to make sense

of this and his body churned out simultaneous waves of horror and confusion. He shook his head hard, as if to fling everything out of it, and chased after himself. Even in his weirdest dreams, he'd never experienced anything so strange and disturbing.

When he reached the other side of the grove, he saw a new ship, much smaller than Clave's, had set down right near the trees.

That's how his double must have arrived. And that's where he was headed now.

Another ship landed, next to it. The hatch opened. Nicholas slid to a halt so fast, he could feel his shoes trying to catch fire. He skittered behind a tree as a gut-wrenching sight brought back horrible memories that had never entirely left his mind and triggered his greatest fear.

Craborzi piled out of the ship. They were small, but there were many of them. Their resemblance to centipedes caused shudders of revulsion to surge through Nicholas's body. That same phobia had caused him to stomp a group of Craborzi to death when he'd rescued Henrietta from them a lifetime ago. The act became known throughout the universe as *The Flamenco Dance of Death*.

Time, exposure to them, and several successful evasions of their attempts to kill him had not weakened this fear in any way. He wrapped his arms around the trunk of the tree.

This can't get any worse, he thought.

It did.

The Craborzi leaped on his double and impaled him with long spears, stabbing him first in the legs to bring him down, and then all over his body as he writhed on the ground and howled in pain.

Nicholas's gasp was masked by the cries of the victim. His stomach lurched at the sight of blood spurting from so many wounds.

The Craborzi, chittering like a swarm of locusts, raised the spears over their heads and carried the wriggling, screaming Nicholas back into their ship.

Nicholas stayed put. They hadn't noticed him. They were too intent on their victim.

He dropped to his knees.

And then, he passed out.

A FADE WORSE
THAN DEATH

There is an Earth saying, "Don't spread yourself too thin." This, I fear, is what is happening to me. Nicholas must feel abandoned. That's terrible. He has so much on his shoulders. He takes the task of emperor too seriously. But that's what makes him a fine young man. And a much finer one than he realizes.

I was unaware for far too long that my voice was growing fainter to him. It sounds the same as always to me. But the clues were there. He had more and more difficulty understanding me. He never even noticed my attempt to warn him about the attack.

The great tragedy is that I am still aware of many things, now that I know what to turn my attention to. It is a tragedy because some of what I see, including the horror he observed with the Craborzi, involves plots against him. There's no way I can warn him. At least, I haven't found a way. Not yet. All I can do is tell the tale, and search for some way to reestablish contact with him before it is too late.

WE'RE DONE!

Nicholas slipped back into consciousness as he was being carried into the ship on Clave's shoulder.

"I saw it from here," Clave said. "You were chasing someone. Who was it?"

"Me . . ." Nicholas said. "I killed them. I mean *he* killed them. Not all. But fifteen of them. The Senbler."

"Actually, you met the Plenith," Clave said as he deposited Nicholas in his seat. "The Senbler live underground. They're plantlike. The Plenith provide them with sensory input. They give the Plenith essential minerals. It's a mutually beneficial relationship."

"What?" Nicholas was more confused than ever. "So the Senbler aren't dead?"

"No. But they might as well be, without their symbiots. They'll be trapped in eternal darkness, alone with their thoughts, stuck with no way to communicate or interact with the outside world." Clave handed Nicholas a water flask. "Here. Drink this."

Nicholas sipped some water, and thought about eternal darkness. He got bored if he had to spend more than thirty seconds doing nothing. Maybe the Senbler's fate was even worse than death. "Bad things happen wherever I go." He struggled to swallow the first sip. The air in the ship felt unbearably heavy.

"It's not your fault," Henrietta said. "The killer might have looked like you, but the killer wasn't you."

"Somehow, I'm sure it is my fault," Nicholas said. "There's one way to find out."

He called up the news.

Stella appeared. After covering the major stories, none of which involved the horrifying destruction of adorable creatures, she said, "And in entertainment news, the brand-new live action program, *The Abominable Emperor,* just debuted to a record audience. Here's a quick look at it."

Nicholas had the brutal opportunity to relive what he'd just lived through. It was even worse watching himself slaughter the Plenith this time, since he knew it was coming. And there was no doubt about the murderer. It was his exact twin. Another wave of dizziness washed over him. He flopped back on the floor.

At the end of the clip, a promo came on for the next episode, showing Nicholas escaping in a shuttle.

"How . . ." Nicholas said. He'd seen his double receive deadly spear thrusts. There was no way he'd be piloting a ship just a few minutes later. "I don't understand . . ."

"Don't pay it any attention," Clave said. "It's just a silly program. Nothing important. Mindless entertainment for the masses."

Nicholas sat up again, moving slowly enough to keep from feeling another wave of dizziness. "But that was *me*! Why would anyone do that?" He looked at Clave. Clave looked at the viewport.

"What are you hiding?" Nicholas asked.

Clave said something very softly.

"What?" Nicholas asked.

Clave spoke a bit more loudly. "I'm afraid it's maybe slightly possible there's a tiny chance they're using clones."

"What? Clones? How?"

As Nicholas gathered his wits together to form a longer sentence, Clave said, "I could be wrong, but I suppose there's a teeny little prospect they used the socks to perhaps potentially get some of your cells."

"What? Who?" Nicholas asked as his efforts to make sense of all this failed.

"That should be obvious," Clave said. He made a gesture like he was poking someone with a spear.

"The Craborzi?" Nicholas asked.

"I'm afraid so," Clave said.

"They bought my socks so they could clone me?" he asked.

"It sort of looks that way," Clave said.

"But that was just a week or two ago," Nicholas said.

"Accelerated growth," Clave said. "The body develops. The mind doesn't. Somehow, they programmed it to become a killer, specifically targeting the Senbler. That must be why it left you alone. You weren't seen as a target. That was lucky for us."

"I'm glad it's over," Nicholas said. "I never want to see anything like that again."

"Neither do I. But we might," Henrietta said. "There could be more clones."

Nicholas tried to picture a room full of himselves. "How many could they make?"

"A lot," Clave said.

Nicholas felt his back and shoulders start to tremble. "How could you?"

"I didn't know the Craborzi would buy the socks," Clave said. "If I had, I would never have sold them. Or the shirt. Or the pen. Or the comic book."

Nicholas thought about things he'd misplaced recently. "So there are parts of me all over the universe?" he asked.

"I doubt anyone else cloned you," Clave said. "You humans are not exactly useful for most purposes."

Nicholas pointed at the area where *The Abominable Emperor* had appeared. "This is all your fault!"

"I'm sorry," Clave said.

"I'm done with you." Nicholas threw his phone to the floor and stomped on it. "I never want to hear from you again."

"But—"

"Send me home," Nicholas shouted as he scooped up Henrietta and stepped into the transporter cage. "We're finished!"

"You won't be able to—"

"Now!" Nicholas screamed.

"As you wish, Emperor." Clave activated the teleporter. "Farewell."

Nicholas felt the falling-in-two-directions sensation, and found himself back in his room. His mother stood in the hallway, her hand on the knob, facing him on the other side of the door she'd obviously just opened. Her jaw dropped.

HOW MANY EMPERORS DOES IT TAKE TO MESS UP A UNIVERSE?

It would not be unreasonable to ask why, in an infinite universe, there are not infinite emperors. The two best answers to that, neither of which is totally satisfying, are that there are indeed infinite emperors but we'll never know about them because they are infinitely far apart, or the answer one encounters to most deep mysteries: we don't know.

In truth, other than satisfying curiosity, the answer doesn't really matter when the reality, based on our own experience, is that there is one emperor.

Though (and there's always a though) there have been times, because of political divisions, rivalries, and the general snittiness of living beings whenever positions of power are involved, when there was more than one emperor. This is no different than the situation on Earth, for example, back in a period starting at 1378, when there were two popes. Examples can be found of two kings or queens.

As far as we know, at the moment, there is just one emperor. And he's not having a very good day.

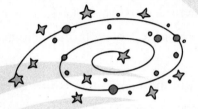

STRANDED

Y ou're getting really good with your magic," his mom said.

"Um . . ." Nicholas was too engulfed in rage to give a coherent reply.

"But don't forget to work on your ventriloquism," she said. "I think that's where you'll really be able to stand out." She flashed him a mommish smile and headed down the hall.

"I can't believe Clave did that," Nicholas said.

"I can," Henrietta said. "Still, he didn't know it would turn out so badly. Though, given the Craborzi are so enthusiastic about science, and about killing things, it's not totally surprising."

"Everyone's going to think I'm a slaughterer," Nicholas said.

Henrietta responded with silence.

"Well, okay. I am sort of a mass killer. And there's already that video of me on the Craborzi ship." Nicholas shuddered, as always, when he remembered the sounds and smells of that violent attack, and pictured the crushed remains of his victims. "But it was all by accident. This was intentional. Those poor creatures. That was so terrible." He crossed the room and fell backward on his bed.

"It was awful," Henrietta said. She crawled from his pocket, walked across his chest to his shoulder, and nuzzled his neck with her head. "But it wasn't you."

"And the clone!" Nicholas shouted as Henrietta's attempt to offer words of comfort made him focus on another victim. He sat up, nearly launching Henrietta across the room. "The poor clone. Poor me. They tortured it with those spears. What for? To make people want to hurt me?"

"Probably. And to get a big audience," Henrietta said.

Nicholas flopped back down.

And then he jolted back up. This time, Henrietta was braced for the sudden move.

"My phone! I smashed my only way to communicate with Clave," Nicholas said.

"I know. I was there."

"And he's my only way off the planet," Nicholas said.

"That seems to be the case," Henrietta said.

"I'll have to wait until somebody comes down to check on me," Nicholas said. "But the Syndics gave an order restricting anyone from coming down here without permission. So I'm stuck on Earth. I can't go into space. I can't go anywhere. There's no way I can prove I didn't murder those poor Plenith. And there's no way I can do anything to stop the Craborzi."

"Maybe you can build something to communicate with Clave or the Syndics," Henrietta suggested. "We saw that in a movie about that alien stranded here. Remember?"

"The only thing I ever built exploded and showered my teachers with rotting pieces of brain," Nicholas said. The memory brought a tiny smile to his face, but it faded quickly as he returned to thoughts of the present and future. "We're trapped here."

"There are worse places to be stuck," Henrietta said. "There's plenty to chew and lots to eat. This is our home. It always has been. On top of that, nobody wants you to solve their problems down here."

"Except Ms. Galendrea." Nicholas smiled again at his own joke. And at the thought of his teacher, which, of course, led to thoughts of Stella. "It would be sort of nice to be just plain old me for a while. Or maybe even forever."

Though he still felt he'd lost something by cutting himself off from Clave, and from space travel, the sense of relief stayed with him all the way until he went to sleep. But his dreams were troubled by images of Craborzi, spears, slaughtered aliens, and dying clones.

The next morning, as he got ready for school, he realized a bit more stress had slipped away from his mind. "I'm looking forward to just being a kid for a while," he told Henrietta.

"Or forever," she said.

"That wouldn't be so bad," Nicholas said. He put Henrietta in his pocket, grabbed his backpack, and headed out the door.

Right now, I'm just a kid, he thought as he took his seat in algebra. He thought about all the power he'd walked—or teleported—away from.

"Whoa!" he said as a revelation hit him.

Ms. Galendrea turned away from the board and shot Nicholas a look that clearly informed him his allowable outbursts for the day were defined by an integer between zero and two. Nicholas slumped down a bit in his seat and shot back an *Oops, sorry* expression. Or, at least, he hoped that's what it conveyed.

"Revelation?" Henrietta asked.

"I could have had Earth destroyed," Nicholas whispered.

"Sure you could," Henrietta said. "You're the emperor. Didn't you already know that?"

"I *knew* it, but I didn't really think about it." Nicholas stopped his whispering as Ms. Galendrea spun around again.

But they picked up the discussion on the way home from school. "I mean, the emperor could destroy any planet he wanted."

"And face the consequences," Henrietta said.

"Sure. But nobody should have that kind of power," he said. "Nobody should ever be able to destroy a whole planet. Or even a whole family."

"If a power exists, someone will probably have it," Henrietta said.

"I have no power, now. Maybe they'll pick a new emperor." Nicholas was surprised to feel a small twinge of jealousy at the idea of having someone take his place. But he was pretty sure he'd be able to adapt to being just a normal kid again.

"Why would they want to replace you?" Henrietta asked. "You're doing a good job."

"No, I'm not. And I'm the worst choice for emperor in the universe. I'm not smart. I'm not clever. And I'm even less useful without Jeef. Nobody should be asking me to solve their problems." Nicholas looked up toward the sky. "I'd give anything to have her back with us."

"So would I," Henrietta said. "But you're smarter than you think. And everyone has doubts. I see it all the time in your school."

"Not everyone," Nicholas said.

"Like who?" Henrietta asked.

Nicholas paused to compile a mental list of the most likely candidates. There were kids in his school who just seemed to glide through life on a frictionless rail. "Jordy Frenbacher," Nicholas said. "He's got straight As since kindergarten. He knows everything."

"And he chews his pencils," Henrietta said. "He's so nervous in class, he nibbles the eraser ends right off of them."

"No he doesn't," Nicholas said.

"Trust me, I know gnawing when I see it," Henrietta said. "And when I hear it. He's very quiet about it, but watch him and you'll see."

"Okay, maybe he's a bit nervous. But Shelly Gower is totally cool. She's like the best-dressed kid in class."

"Did you ever notice that she leans deep into her locker when she's getting her books?" Henrietta asked.

"No. Yeah. Sorta," Nicholas said. "So what?"

"That's when she cries," Henrietta said.

"Cries?" Nicholas asked.

"Yes. Sadly, I can hear it. And I can smell the tears. Nobody notices that, either," Henrietta said.

"Why?" Nicholas asked. "What could she possibly be sad about?"

"I have no idea," Henrietta said. "I suspect there could be infinite reasons."

"I never would have guessed," Nicholas said. "Now, I feel bad for her."

"That's what makes you a good emperor," Henrietta said. "There's really only one person you aren't always nice to."

"Who?" He started to compile another mental list.

"Yourself," Henrietta said. "Give the emperor a break."

"I'll try," Nicholas said. "And I'll definitely take a break."

When he got home, he found his parents waiting for him in the living room.

"We have to talk," his mom said.

"This is serious," his dad said.

This is trouble, Nicholas thought.

"Our manager just called," his mom said. "We're booked for two days of concerts in Spokane. The group that was supposed to do the shows couldn't make it."

"They were coming from Scotland," his dad said. "But their airline canceled all flights. They're out of fuel. Bad news for the Scottish players."

"But good news for us," his mom said. "The pay is great. The problem is, your uncle and aunt can't come stay with you. We called them both. No luck."

His dad stared at him. "We need to leave you alone for two nights. And we need to know we can trust you."

"Totally," Nicholas said. The thought of getting another chance to prove himself made him smile.

"Don't look too happy," his mom said. "This is serious."

Nicholas killed his smile. "I know. You can trust me. I won't . . ." He closed his mouth before he could add *destroy any more planets.* Then he opened it long enough to end his sentence with something safer. ". . . do anything bad. And it's only two days. That's hardly any time at all."

His dad nodded. So did his mom.

"You'll keep me out of trouble?" he asked Henrietta on his way up to his room.

"I'll try my best," she said.

"That's all I can ask."

His parents headed out for Spokane early the next morning. Nicholas found a note on the fridge. *Keep closed!!!*

"Like I'd make the same mistake twice," he said as he opened the fridge and grabbed the milk for his cereal.

His day turned interesting soon after that.

"Want to study together for the test?" Stella asked as Nicholas was leaving algebra.

"Sure!" Nicholas said. He was relieved that his reply, though slightly louder than necessary, had somehow managed to be delivered at a pitch low enough that humans could hear it and nearby pieces of glass wouldn't shatter.

"Great," Stella said. "My folks are getting the rugs cleaned. How about we go to your place?"

Nicholas caught himself this time before blurting an immediate response, and managed to issue a much more restrained version of, "Sure."

His ability to concentrate on his classes was even more fragile than usual. He tried to think of every possible aspect of the study session, from providing acceptable snacks to making sure there were no embarrassing parental possessions within sight of the kitchen table.

After school, they headed toward his house.

"I told you where I'd go if I could go anywhere," Stella said. "My turn to ask. What would you do if you could accomplish anything?"

"Stop all wars," Nicholas said without even thinking. He paused to consider his words, and decided they weren't going to reveal his secret, unlike the time he'd blurted something out at his parents. Not that Stella would be any more likely to believe him than his parents were.

She didn't respond immediately. Nicholas got the impression she was giving his words serious thought. He was tempted to add something like, "Just kidding," to let her know he didn't really think some kid from Yelm could actually make that happen, but he decided to wait.

"That's ambitious," she finally said. "But a good choice."

"Thanks."

"How would you do it?" she asked.

He was beginning to wish he'd said something more deeply rooted in fantasy, like, "Win the Super Bowl," which wouldn't have required further questions. All he could think to say was, "I don't know."

"You'd have to have some kind of influence or power," she said.

Nicholas decided this was a good time to change the subject. "Ever been to Spokane?"

"No. Not yet," Stella said. "Have you?"

"Nope."

They chatted about other places they hadn't been as they finished the walk. When they got to the kitchen, Nicholas grabbed a bag of pretzels, a bag of cheese puffs, a bag of plain potato chips, a bag of sour cream and onion potato chips, and a bag of popcorn from a cabinet.

"Snack?" he asked.

Stella laughed, but not in a mean way. "It would be rude to refuse."

Nicholas was beginning to suspect that she actually enjoyed his company. Or, at least, found it pleasantly amusing.

The unfamiliar sound, masked at first by the crunch

of tandem jaws grinding at various carbohydrates, trickled into his consciousness less than five minutes after he and Stella had taken seats at the kitchen table, which was a pretty good trick for any sound to pull off given that 200 percent of Nicholas's attention was focused on Stella. He'd given 100 percent to admiring her, and another 100 percent to trying not to do or say anything that would reveal how hopeless he was in social situations.

"Do you hear something?" he whispered to Henrietta, who'd been lazily chewing at the edge of a piece of scrap paper.

"Definitely," she said.

Nicholas tried to turn his attention back to Stella. But the trickle grew to a hum, and then to a buzz. As it reached whatever lay between a buzz and a roar, Nicholas walked to the living room and glanced out the front window. That's when he saw the leading edge of the murderous mob that was charging down the street toward his house.

His first idle thought, *I wonder where they're going,* was quickly replaced by the knowledge that if there was a mob charging anywhere near him, and especially if that mob was heading in his general direction, he was almost certainly the target.

It didn't seem wise to wait there and see whether he was right.

"Run!" he screamed to Stella. He scrambled back to the kitchen, snatched up Henrietta, and pointed toward the back door.

FAKE NEWS!

No spacecraft unaffiliated with the emperor could approach Earth without triggering an alarm that was being monitored by Clave. But a small drone vessel disguised as a meteor could slip past the orbiting sensors undetected. Even that, if it had come close to Nicholas's home, would have been destroyed by defensive systems the Syndics had put in place. But this drone didn't need to be near Nicholas's house, or even make planetfall. It just needed to get within range of a communications satellite. Once there, it captured the broadcast signal for the seven most popular networks in the region and fed the residents of Nicholas's city and other nearby locations a breaking news story about the theft of the world's petroleum.

The newscaster, a Kroxilanium chosen for his resemblance to an Earthling, broke the story:

"We have just learned that the loss of oil resources that has brought surging fuel prices, a plastics shortage, and other turmoil to all of Earth was orchestrated by one individual."

A photo of Nicholas appeared, showing him standing near his house. The house number and street sign were clearly visible. Anyone with even the slightest ability to search the internet could immediately get directions to Nicholas's house.

More than a few viewers decided to take the law, and revenge, into their own hands. They also took rakes, shovels, baseball bats, and various other blunt weapons of small destruction into those angry petroleum-deprived hands.

Individuals, small groups, and the entire staff of one electronics store, which happened to see the story simultaneously on seventy-eight large-screen televisions, headed toward Nicholas's house, in search of vengeance.

Teritus, who had conspired against the more moderate of the Unilluminated while falsely presenting his own moderate stand, was pleased. He already had a new candidate in place, ready to become emperor of the universe immediately after the short reign, and sudden, violent death, of Nicholas Landrew.

MOB, SEEN

As they raced up the hill, Nicholas heard a roar from the left. A motorcycle sped toward them, kicking back tufts of grass as its rear wheel spun on the uneven ground. The driver was holding a baseball bat in one hand.

This is it, he thought. The emperor was about to get swatted out of existence.

As the motorcycle zoomed toward them, Nicholas reached to push Stella out of the way. But she sprang clear of his reach, leaped in the air, and spun around, taking the rider off the cycle with a kick. The motorcycle sped past them, riderless.

"What . . . ?" Nicholas gasped as Stella came to a graceful landing next to him.

"Ballet," she said. "Ten years of classes. I guess my mom was right that it would be good for me."

Nicholas stared. Stella grabbed his arm with one hand and tugged. "Come on. I can't dance my way through that whole mob."

"Yeah. Right." Nicholas followed her up the hill.

As the mob closed in on Nicholas, he heard a terrifying roar from farther up the hill. This one, unlike that of the motorcycle, was not mechanical. He looked ahead and almost screamed. A grizzly bear, standing fully reared up on its hind legs, towered over them. After a second roar, it dropped to all fours and charged. His mind almost spun out of control dealing with the reality that he was caught between two different tragic endings.

Stella dropped into a stance, looking like she was ready to throw a kick at the beast.

That's when the bear winked at him.

And that's when he noticed the slightest rainbow shimmer dancing around the outlines of the beast.

"It's okay," he told Stella. "The bear won't hurt us."

The mob, on the other hand, was totally decisive about their best option. They fled.

Once the mob was safely out of sight, Nicholas approached the bear.

"Miss me?" Clave asked as he switched off the holographic disguise.

Nicholas tried to answer, but ended up nodding as he pulled air back into his lungs and waited for his pulse to slow down to the point where it actually had a bit of space between beats.

"Let's get to the ship," Clave said. "I'm sure some of your fellow barbarians are enraged enough to decide they can tackle a bear."

"Good idea." Nicholas looked over at Stella. "Come on. It's safe."

As more mob sounds rumbled in the distance, the group headed for the other side of the ridge, where Clave had docked *The Nick of Space*.

"Is that what I think it is?" Stella asked when the hatch opened.

"Yup," Nicholas said. "It sure is." He led her up the ramp.

"Where are we going?" she asked.

Nicholas grinned. "Wherever we want."

"You probably want this," Clave said, handing Nicholas a phone. "I managed to repair the damage you did before you stormed away. They really should call you

Emperor Stompy, seeing how that seems to be your favorite method of destroying things." Clave stomped his own foot for emphasis.

"Um, thanks," Nicholas said. "And thanks for saving us."

"You're welcome," Clave said.

"I'm sorry I got so angry with you," Nicholas said.

"You're forgiven."

Nicholas waited to see if Clave would offer any sort of apology for selling his socks. But Clave just took a seat at the console and said, "We should leave here before they make their next charge. I don't think the barbarians are quite ready to discover how insignificant they are."

Nicholas pointed to the second seat. "You'll want to strap in," he told Stella.

He took Henrietta from his pocket, cradled her to his chest, and sat on the floor between Clave and Stella.

"We're really going into space?" Stella asked.

"Yup."

After they'd lifted off, Nicholas brought up the news. As emperor, he felt a bit of responsibility to see what was going on in his realm, even if he'd enjoyed being totally out of touch for the brief period when he was stranded on Earth. And he was hoping the interest in the Craborzi reality show had faded away. But he realized he had one much more immediate concern.

During the broadcast, Nicholas almost broke his neck looking between the ideal news construct, Stella Astrallis, and his pretty amazing classmate, Stella Galendrea. His classmate was totally absorbed by whatever she was seeing.

Maybe her newscaster looks like me, he thought. There was a nice symmetry to that possibility, though Nicholas hadn't seen much evidence that the universe cared for his theories in such matters. Or any matters, for that matter.

He waited for Stella G. to glance at him in surprise at the coincidence, while still keeping one eye on Stella A. She didn't. When the newscast ended, Stella let out a dreamy sigh.

"Who'd you see?" Nicholas asked.

"A guy on a horse." She grinned, as if savoring the memory.

"Horse?" Nicholas asked.

"Yeah. A beautiful Arabian. I don't know why he'd be sitting on a horse to give the news, but he looked pretty cool." She glanced toward the empty space where the news had appeared, then looked back at Nicholas and said, "Why did you ask? Do people see different things?"

"Yeah," Nicholas said. He could feel his face starting to flush in anticipation of her next question.

"Who did you see?" Stella asked.

"A woman. No horse," Nicholas said. He took a deep breath and hoped that was the end of the conversation. He really didn't want their discussion to stroll any further down that dangerous road. Happily, Stella turned her attention to the viewport.

"Earth . . ." she said. "It's so beautiful."

Her gasp reminded Nicholas of the first time he'd spotted Earth from space. And it reminded him that whatever else happened, their next move would be a nice surprise for Stella.

DID HE PLAN IT
THAT WAY?

While Nicholas only toyed with the idea that he could destroy Earth, or possibly just the idea that he could have that idea, more than a few emperors acted on that thought and had their home planet destroyed. Most notably, Glute the Mindless, who got distracted immediately after giving the order, forgot about it, and failed to leave the planet. Glute's reasons for wanting the destruction in the first place are not known. And even if they were known, they might not make much sense.

Gevlar the Dreadful destroyed all sentient life on his home planet, Ragi II, for what seemed, to him, to be the best of all possible reasons. His fellow Ragites were constantly at war with each other. While this solution was briefly effective, pillagers from three other planets attempted to take control of Ragi. So Gevlar wiped out all sentient life on those three planets. This expanding process, truly a vicious circle, or outward spiral, repeated several more times, earning Gevlar a reputation as a warlord, before he himself was wiped out in an attempt to stop more wars.

Frebmuch the Vagabond destroyed his home planet because everybody in his town made fun of him when he was young. Apparently, he found the experience of revenge so satisfying that he looked for another planet where he would be made fun of. After living there briefly, he had that planet destroyed. This pattern continued until he'd destroyed seventeen planets. By then, the pattern became obvious enough that the next planet he was planning to move to destroyed him. Nobody objected to this.

There are countless other examples. But our tour is about to start, so let's get on board.

A FAMILIAR RING

Nicholas had spent a lot of time trying to decide whether it would be more impressive to watch Saturn grow larger in the viewport as they approached it, or to flip on the viewport once they got close, and dazzle Stella with a sudden view of the rings, and the sudden realization that he had granted her seemingly impossible wish.

He ran the question past Henrietta while Stella was distracted watching the dwindling view of Earth.

"Think about your own experiences," Henrietta said.

"I saw Earth suddenly, from the Craborzi ship. And Clave surprised me with a view of my first jump node. It was cloaked until you got close. I've seen a bunch of planets during slow approaches." He thought back to his reactions. The answer was pretty obvious.

"Sudden appearance," he'd said. That had made the most dramatic impression on him.

And so, when he whispered their destination to Clave, he'd asked him to keep the viewport switched to the rear image.

"Where are we going?" Stella asked, after Earth had dwindled to a small disk.

"It's a surprise," Nicholas said. He suspected she'd totally forgotten his question about where in the universe she'd want to go.

"How about a clue?" she asked.

Nicholas, who had never been very good at making up clues, was afraid he'd give away the surprise if he said anything at all, so he just smiled and shook his head. He thought about letting her see the jump node, but there'd be plenty more of those to see. He didn't want anything to detract from her first look at Saturn.

"Hold on," he said when he saw they were about to jump.

A few minutes later, Clave said to Stella, "Come over here by the bulkhead."

Stella went over. Nicholas followed her.

Clave nodded at Nicholas. Nicholas nodded back. "Behold," he said.

The viewport switched to the forward image. Saturn appeared. Stella gasped and grabbed Nicholas's hand. "It's . . ." Her eyes glistened like moons in the reflected light of the giant planet.

"Yeah, I know," Nicholas said.

His pulse raced as her grip grew tighter. Then, she released his hand and clasped both her hands in front of her, as if she could barely contain her joy.

Nicholas watched her glowing face and waited until she'd seen her fill.

"That was incredible," she said. "It was even more amazing than I'd ever dreamed it could be. Thank you."

"You're welcome," Nicholas said.

"Now what?" she asked.

"Good question," Nicholas said. "We should probably stay away from Earth for a while, until people get tired of waiting for me to show up so they can kill me."

"What did you do?" Stella asked.

"Long story," Nicholas said.

Stella settled on the floor of the cabin. "Well, you did say we should wait a while."

Nicholas sat opposite her and gave Henrietta a

friendly pat. "It all started when Henrietta disappeared in a flash of purple light."

He told her the tale, watching her face the whole time to see whether she believed him, and more importantly, whether she would understand that none of the horrible things that had happened on his road to becoming emperor of the universe were the result of bad or evil decisions on his part. He didn't share too many details about Jeef. The memories made him sad.

Stella listened without interrupting. Clave broke in a few times with throat clearings or other interruptions when it was obvious he felt his part in all of this, both as a participant and as a chronicler of events, had not been given enough glory.

Henrietta stayed silent, except to speak in front of Stella for the first time when Nicholas got to the part of the story where she gained sentience.

"It's true," she said.

Stella seemed only mildly surprised by this.

Jeef remained, sadly, out of touch.

"And that's how we got where we are, and why we should probably stay off-planet for a little while," Nicholas said.

"That's quite a story," Stella said.

"Do you believe me?" Nicholas asked.

She laughed. "Of course I believe you. We're in a spaceship. I just saw the rings of Saturn. And everything you told me had the ring of truth to it."

Nicholas smiled at her joke. And more so at her faith in him. But he realized there might be a problem. "My parents are out of town for a couple days. I won't get in trouble if I'm not home. But what about you?"

"My parents are away, too," Stella said.

"That's quite a coincidence," Nicholas said.

Stella gave him an odd look. "Not really."

"What do you mean?" Nicholas asked.

She looked away from him, then glanced back several times, as if making a major decision.

"It's my turn for a story," she finally said. "But not a very long one. I'm not who I seem to be."

Oh boy, Nicholas thought. He glanced at the hand she'd recently held, then settled down, hoping that the girl of his dreams wasn't about to reveal she was actually part of a nightmare.

WILL WONDERS
NEVER CEASE?

While there is a planet where the trees sing, they only know three songs. And while there are birds that leave colored trails behind them as they fly, those trails are made of a methane mixture so nauseating that it can kill insects and silence even the most enthusiastic singing tree. *Wonders* are very much a personal thing, as Stella's fulfilled wish demonstrates.

Even beyond personal wishes, there are vast differences among species that make certain experiences more or less desirable. A race that doesn't perceive sound waves will have no interest in singing trees, no matter how many tunes they might produce, and a race with no sense of smell will be delighted by the stench-free sight of colorful trails behind those birds.

While there are very few, if any, universal wonders, there are countless wonders that appeal to a specific audience. The Flufferpen, for example, are essentially soap bubbles. Though "soap" isn't entirely accurate. Their film is a bit more durable. But they glisten with rainbow shimmers like soap bubbles, and float on the wind in enthralling ways. They also are able to generate a potentially lethal charge of electricity and shoot it at anyone or anything that greatly annoys them.

Fortunately, Flufferpen are highly tolerant. There are only three recorded cases where someone actually annoyed a Flufferpen enough to get zapped. One of those unfortunate lightning rods was the late great stand-up comic, Shucks McChuckles, who barely survived the jolt. This rarity has led to a popular challenge among beings who enjoy annoying others. Tourists flock to Flufferp in the hopes of being the fourth entity in recorded history to succeed in annoying a Flufferpen enough to get zapped by their charge.

KILLER EYES

'm not human," Stella said.

Nicholas ran his eyes over her from head to toe, and then back. He couldn't imagine any being that was more human than the girl who sat in front of him.

"I'm humanoid," Stella said. "Very similar. I was selected because my bosses believed I would be attractive to you. Were they right?"

Nicholas attempted to speak, managed to gulp and clear his throat, then gave up all attempts to find a means of denial and nodded.

"I thought so," she said. "My bosses are very smart."

"Who are they?" Henrietta asked.

"That's a secret," Stella said.

"Jeef?" Nicholas asked, out of habit. The silence he

got in return tugged at his heart. He missed Jeef even more than he'd missed his phone.

"I was sent here to keep an eye on you, and to make sure you didn't make any moves or set in motion any policies that went against the wishes of my bosses," Stella said.

"So you were spying on me?" Nicholas asked. He felt the same beginning tingle of the rush of anger that had caused him to stomp his phone, but he managed to control it this time. He didn't want to be angry with her.

"Basically," she said.

"Spying on me . . ." he repeated.

"Yup."

Nicholas thought about the way she'd taken out that attacker on the motorcycle. "And if I did things your bosses didn't want, what were you supposed to do?"

"Kill you," she said, in as matter-of-fact a way as if she'd just told him what time it was or where she'd put his coat.

A trickle of fear replaced the lingering anger. Nicholas, still on the floor, scooted away from her. "Have I gone against their wishes?"

"Sort of," she said. "Well, actually more than sort of. They want more war, not less."

He pictured her leaping up and delivering a fatal kick to his head. "Are you planning to kill me?"

"Not at the moment," she said. "Getting chased by a bloodthirsty mob gave me a bit of a new perspective on things. So did getting to know you."

"Wait," Nicholas said. "Ms. Galendrea told the class that you're her cousin. Does that mean she isn't human, either?"

"Yeah," Stella said, as if this information, too, was nothing exceptional. "That's exactly what it means."

"She's an alien?" Nicholas asked.

"All algebra teachers are," Stella said. "Our ancient ancestors created an impenetrable form of math that only we could teach. That's allowed us to spread throughout the universe. We're like the mathematical version of wind-borne seeds. Oh, dear . . ."

"What?" Nicholas asked.

"That was definitely too much information. I really should kill you now." She glanced over at Clave, and then at Henrietta. "All of you, actually. It would be terrible if our secret got out. But I really don't want to show up on the news as a notorious assassin. I kind of like living on Earth. And you are just too cute to kill," she said, reaching out to give Henrietta a skritch on the head.

The mention of news revived the other Stella, who started another report triggered by the keywords the young Stella had spoken. "A new episode of *Nicholas the Assassin* has horrified and outraged viewers across the universe. Speculation is running high that this is more than just an entertainment series."

A video appeared of Nicholas running toward a group of adorable birds, holding a flame thrower. The birds stared at their attacker, blinking and craning their necks, but didn't seem to know enough to run until it was too late.

"No!" Nicholas screamed at himself. He wanted to turn away, but he couldn't rip his eyes from the horror show. Like before, after the clone slaughtered his victims, a ship appeared and Craborzi apprehended him. This time, instead of spears, they blew his legs off with expertly flung mini grenades, and then picked him up by his flailing arms and carried him to their ship. Before they'd even moved out of view, the flailing arms drooped and the head slumped to the side.

The screams rang in Nicholas's ears as the image faded. A wave of nausea surged through his body, followed by rage he made no effort to suppress.

"How many times am I going to see myself slaughter innocent creatures?" he screamed. "How many times am I going to see myself get murdered?"

"Clones," Clave told Stella.

"How many do you think there are?" Nicholas asked. "The Craborzi aren't going to stop after only two episodes."

"No idea," Clave said. "There could be a dozen. There could be thousands."

"Thousands?" Nicholas asked.

"Let's hope not," Clave said.

"We have to rescue them," Nicholas said. "We can't let the Craborzi keep doing this to them."

"They're not really human," Clave said.

"Yes they are!" Nicholas shouted. "They're me."

"They don't have your memories. They don't have your thoughts," Clave said. "They're blank slates, force-grown to maturity, and then given a task."

"But they're capable of thoughts, right?" Nicholas asked.

"Sure," Clave said. "They have functioning brains. They've just been kept away from any stimulus until they're needed."

"They can think and feel. They're as human as I am. We're saving them." Nicholas looked over at Stella, whose face had grown quite pale for that of a trained assassin. "Right?"

"We have to," Stella said.

Nicholas glanced down at Henrietta.

"Of course," she said. "It's the right thing to do."

This time, as he glanced up at the ceiling, he caught himself before he asked for Jeef's opinion. Even that slight slip reminded him of his loss. He turned back to his companions. "So how do we find them?" Nicholas asked.

Stella and Henrietta both shrugged in their unique but equally adorable ways. Actually, the fact that one of them was capable of killing Nicholas did push her down slightly in his rankings of adorability, but she still held a firm grip on second place. And while *adorable* might have lost a few points, *awesome* had moved up to fill the gap.

Nicholas looked at Clave, who had not yet joined the others in voicing his support for a rescue.

Clave looked away.

"Do you know something?" Nicholas asked.

Clave didn't answer.

"Tell me," Nicholas said.

"If I tell you, you are going to do something very dangerous and stupid," Clave said. "And, based on past experience, that means I'm also going to do something very dangerous and stupid, because I can't let you do dangerous and stupid things alone. And this time, we might not be as lucky as we were in the past. You can only achieve the impossible so many times before the odds catch up with you."

"I'm okay with that," Nicholas said. "First, we should drop Stella off somewhere safe."

"Oh, you want to save the little woman?" Stella poked Nicholas in the shoulder with a finger that felt just slightly less dangerous than a steel rod, completely assassinating the glow of chivalry he'd felt when he'd made that statement.

"I just wanted to . . ." He let his sentence fade away. He had no idea whether there was any correct response to her question.

"Protect the girl? Is that what you're saying?" she asked. "You big, brawny masculine brutes will charge into the face of danger while I stay home, embroidering petticoats?"

"No!" Nicholas yelled, blurting out the necessary lie as he tried to think of another explanation for his suggestion. As his shout died the death that all false words are vulnerable to, his mind failed to come up with anything better. Partly by accident, and partly by essentially being a decent human being, he abandoned his search for justification, and came up instead with the right response.

"I'm sorry. That was wrong."

"Apology accepted," Stella said.

"Would you like to come with us on a highly dangerous mission and possibly die or get captured by horrible creatures who might slowly peel away your flesh and remove your other organs while your heart keeps beating and your mind remains fully aware?" Nicholas asked.

Stella flashed him a steely grin. "I thought you'd never ask."

"Great." Nicholas turned back to Clave. "So, where are these clones being kept?"

"Watch this." Clave pulled up the horrible video of the cloned Nicholas getting brutally captured.

Nicholas flinched and put his hands up, blocking the image. "I really don't need to see that again."

"Wait," Clave said. "You need to see the part after the scene ends. They cut this off for the news, but it's in the actual broadcast."

Nicholas waited. He kept his eyes half closed until the credits rolled, blurring the terrible events in the video. At the end of the credits, right above the words *A Cloud*

Mansion II Intergalactic Production, was a line for *Technical advisor and clone programmer: Morglob Sputum.*

"Morglob!" Henrietta said.

"Ewww," Nicholas said. Just hearing that name made him feel like skipping his next five meals. "But we blew up his home." Nicholas thought back to the moment when he saw Morglob's *Cloud Mansion Intergalactic* begin to break apart.

"Apparently, he had at least one other one available," Clave said.

"And we launched him into space," Nicholas added. "I didn't see any shuttles leave when we destroyed his mansion."

"I believe Phleghmhackians can survive the brutality of outer space," Clave said. "Somehow, he managed to get rescued. I'd imagine he'd be very enthusiastic about getting revenge on you for blowing up his home."

"It wasn't my idea," Nicholas said. Spott had tricked him and Clave into helping trigger the self-destruct mechanism as a way to escape from Morglob, who'd forced him into servitude. "Though I'm glad it happened. He deserved it. I didn't know he could program clones."

"Think about those musicians," Henrietta said.

"Xlotol?" Nicholas said. When he'd first seen the spider-like creatures jabbing each other with sticks and screeching like howler monkeys, he'd thought they were at war. But it turned out they were one of the most popular musical acts in the universe.

"Right," Henrietta said. "They couldn't think on their own. But Morglob could give them orders. He must have approached the Craborzi. This whole plot is based on entertainment, and the fact that so many impressionable minds have a hard time separating fiction from reality. Morglob would want to control every aspect of this, to make sure he got his revenge. The rest of the clones have to be with him."

"That makes sense," Nicholas said. "But how do we find him?"

"We ask an expert," Clave said.

"Like who?" Nicholas asked.

Clave fiddled with the navigation controls. "Like our Beradaxian friend who was his servant for far too many years."

"Spott!" Nicholas said. His whole universe brightened at the thought of paying a visit to his friend. While nothing could mend the hole made by the absence of Jeef, the thought of seeing Spott cheered him up. "That's great. Stella, you'll love Beradaxia. If you think Saturn was amazing, wait until you see the waterfalls and canyons on that planet. Let's go there, Clave!"

"I'm already preparing for the jumps," Clave said.

CLONESPIRACY

The absence of Morglob from the entertainment scene had left a void that was quickly filled. It should be noted that the old Earth saying, "Nature abhors a vacuum," is pretty absurd, given the percent of the universe that is, indeed, vacuous. But there are some voids that are rapidly filled. And this was one of them. His clients were quickly snatched up by other agents. Despite many of them signing horribly exploitive contracts, every single one of them was better off than they'd been with Morglob.

This loss of clients, power, and fame only added to Morglob's rage. He knew he was powerless to get revenge on his own. And he knew that the Craborzi, while not powerless, had failed to find a suitable way to punish the emperor for the brutal deaths he'd visited on the stars of their favorite program, *Let's Cut Things Up!* They were immediately receptive when Morglob, the enemy of their enemy, contacted them with a plan. They didn't even care that the agreement gave him 100 percent of the profits from both the broadcast and any associated merchandise, including the already popular Abominable Emperor Rip Apart Action Figure.

Morglob was not at all surprised when *The Abominable Emperor* became an immediate success throughout the universe. He knew his audience, and never underestimated their thirst for violence. Opinions were divided on whether it was real, despite the fact that it was clearly presented as entertainment and not news. But that didn't seem to matter to the viewers. Either way, they loved to despise the villain at the center of the tale. There's a nearly universal appeal to seeing the powerful get destroyed.

SPOTT ON

S pott was as thrilled to see his friends as they were to see him. And he welcomed the newest member of their group with typical Beradaxian hospitality. He even stood there patiently while Clave recorded a sfumble. He was less thrilled when he learned the reason for their visit.

"So Morglob is out there trying to destroy your reputation, and possibly inspire others to harm you," Spott said. "And you need to find him so you can rescue these clones who would otherwise suffer a horrible death."

"That pretty much covers it," Nicholas said. "Do you have any idea where he might have kept his backup mansion?"

"Let me think about it," Spott said. "I'm sure it will be someplace that is the best or greatest of its kind in the universe in some way. He was all about that. Everything was flash and show for him."

Nicholas felt a mini shudder pass through him as he remembered the door to Morglob's office was decorated with rare and horribly expensive living eyes.

"What's the flashiest place in the universe?" Stella asked.

"Depends on who you ask," Spott said. "But the sector where Morglob had his original home was a good candidate. It made sense he built his first mansion there. We just need to think about similar places."

"This would be so much easier if we could ask Jeef," Nicholas said.

"She's not around?" Spott asked.

"No." That was as much as Nicholas could manage to say. It hurt too much to talk about it. He let Clave fill in the details.

"We'll just have to do our best," Spott said after he'd heard the story. "Let's see what we can come up with."

"We can use the ship's resources," Clave said.

After Clave and Spott went off, Stella asked Nicholas, "Who is Jeef? I heard Clave say she's not around, but who is she?"

"The best cow in the universe," Nicholas said. He took a moment to swallow the sorrow that threatened to close his throat, and then managed to answer her question. It still hurt a lot, but somehow he found it easier to talk about his adventures with Jeef than about her disappearance.

"I can see why you miss her," Stella said when he was finished. "But don't give up hope."

"I won't," Nicholas said. "Hey, they'll probably be gone for a while. Want to see the sights?"

"I'd love to."

Nicholas scooped up Henrietta and then took Stella on a quick tour of the city. By the time they came back, Spott and Clave had returned. They'd narrowed the location of Morglob's mansion down to five strong possibilities.

After they listed them, Nicholas said, "Wait, I'm the emperor. Can't I just send my forces to those places and have them rescue the clones?"

"What forces?" Clave asked.

"Don't I have forces?" Nicholas asked.

"Did you establish forces?" Clave asked.

"I didn't know I had to," Nicholas said. "I just sort of assumed they came with the whole emperor thing. You know—part of the package."

"That's not how it works," Clave said. "Every emperor is so different as far as what they want or need, the Syndics pretty much press RESET whenever a new emperor comes along."

"They did the things I asked about, before," Nicholas said. "They removed the petroleum from Earth." Nicholas realized that was another example of his good intentions having a bad result. Hopefully, this one would be temporary, and not deadly.

"They had that equipment available," Clave said. "And you made it a condition of accepting the offer to become emperor. There is no clone-rescue commando team awaiting your orders. You could request one, but it would take time to get organized."

"I guess we just need to go look for ourselves," Nicholas said.

"I'm coming with you," Spott said.

"It's dangerous," Nicholas said. "The Craborzi might be there."

"I'm your best chance of getting into the mansion and rescuing those clones," Spott said. "I can tell Morglob you'd abducted me and forced me to help you destroy his original home."

"Why would he believe that?" Clave said.

"I'll flatter him," Spott said. "I'll tell him I couldn't

bear to be away from him after living so long in his magnificent presence."

"He'll fall for that?" Clave asked.

"He might be able to survive in a vacuum or in frigid temperatures, but he is totally defenseless against flattery," Spott said. "He's a narcissist. He's pretty much incapable of believing he isn't the best at everything. He'll eagerly swallow anything that reinforces that belief. Praise is his weakness."

"It sounds like we have a plan," Nicholas said. He turned to Stella. "I really want to show you around more of Beradaxia, beyond the city. This planet is amazing. But the Craborzi could be killing the next clone, and a bunch more victims, at any time. And my parents will be back soon. They'll be totally furious if I'm not there when they arrive. I really can't get in more trouble with them. They'll ground me for life."

"They'd ground the emperor?" she asked.

"They don't know about any of this," Nicholas said.

Stella stared at him and blinked. "Seriously?"

"I tried to tell them, but they didn't believe me. I even had Henrietta talk to them. Now, they think I want to be a ventriloquist."

"Parents," Stella said, letting out a sigh. "I don't know

how anyone manages to grow into an adult. And I don't understand how they can totally forget what it's like to be a kid as soon as they get there."

"Roach brains!" Nicholas shouted. He pulled his phone from his pocket.

"What's wrong?" Stella asked.

"I should warn my parents about the mob."

"They're probably gone by now," Stella said. "Mobs have short attention spans."

"I can't take that chance."

Before he could call his parents, they called him.

For the first time in as long as he could remember, instead of letting them leave a voice message, which he would respond to later by means of a text, he answered the call.

"Hi." It felt weird speaking to them on the phone.

"Hi," his mom said. "We're not checking up on you. We're just calling to say hi."

"I know."

"Is everything all right?" she asked.

"Not really."

"Oh, good. Wait! Did you say not really? What happened?"

"Well, the news got out that I was responsible for removing all of Earth's petroleum. So a mob came to the house. Stella and I—" He cut himself off, not wanting to confess to that part, but quickly resumed so he could get the whole story in. "I was chased, but Clave—you remember I mentioned him?—saved me and scared off the mob by using a holographic projection that made him look like an enormous bear. I think it's probably safe to go home after your concert. But you might want to stop down the block to make sure nobody is waiting there before you pull into the driveway."

His mom laughed. "You have such a vivid imagination. Is this a story you're writing for school? If so, you might want to think about cutting it down a bit. You don't want to throw too many unbelievable things at the reader all at once. But I'm glad everything is okay. Sleep well. We'll see you tomorrow."

"Wait. You need to—"

The call ended. "She didn't believe me," Nicholas said.

Stella patted his arm. "Someday, she will."

"Well, we'd better get going," Clave said. "We have a lot of places to check."

They found *Cloud Mansion Intergalactic II* on their third attempt, in orbit around a frozen planet that contained four sets of rings.

Nicholas managed to keep from pointing out to

Stella how much more amazing this was than Saturn. But that did raise a question in his mind.

"You came to Earth from another planet," he said. "You traveled across the universe, probably from another galaxy. Why would you want to see Saturn?"

"Just because I'm an alien doesn't mean I've been much of anywhere," she said. "Until I was assigned this mission, I'd never left home. For me, Saturn was a big deal. Thank you for taking me there." She put a hand on his shoulder and gave it a gentle squeeze.

"Sure." Nicholas felt his face grow warm. "It was nothing. I'm glad I could do it. You were really surprised, weren't you? Saturn is actually pretty cool. I'm so glad I took you there." He forced himself to stop babbling, but he couldn't tear his eyes away from her smile.

Before the silence between Nicholas and Stella could grow too drippily romantic, Clave cleared his throat far more loudly than any throat ever needed and muttered, "Who took you there?"

"Thank you, too, Clave," Stella said. "You're a wonderful pilot."

"You're welcome." Clave brought the ship to a stop far enough away that the enormous structure of *Cloud Mansion II* only filled three-fourths of the view screen.

"I'll keep us out of range of his tractor beam until we see how he reacts to Spott."

Spott sat at the console and spoke. "Hi, Morglob. Um, this is Spott. Your servant. Remember me?"

There was silence for a moment, and then the sickening burbling sound that a large cluster of mucus would make if it spoke through a tube.

"I do. You destroyed my home. Traitor. After all I did for you."

"No! It wasn't me. It was that murdering scoundrel Nicholas the Assassin. You, of all people, should know how evil he is. Everyone knows. He's the worst person in the universe. And he's painfully stupid. You offered to make him a star, and he turned you down. I just can't believe he refused an offer from the greatest agent in the universe. Not just the greatest agent—the greatest living being. He and his henchmen abducted me, but I managed to escape because I needed to come back home. Nobody ever treated me better than you. I am so grateful. I miss you so much."

Nice touch, Nicholas thought, when he heard Spott referring to the mansion as his home.

"Well, you did seem to have a knack for dredging the gristle out of me after a meal," Morglob said.

"It was a pleasure," Spott said.

Nicholas noticed that Spott's whole body had shuddered as he spoke those words. He figured it was only the singer's long years of training that allowed him to keep his disgust out of his voice.

"Who's with you?" Morglob asked.

"Nobody. I stole the ship," Spott said.

"Wonderful. Move closer, and I'll have my scurvy crew latch onto the ship with the tractor beam and bring you in," Morglob said.

Spott glanced at Clave and mouthed the words *Scurvy crew?*

Clave shrugged and mouthed the words *No idea.*

"I'm coming home, Morglob, thanks to your legendary generosity." Spott switched off the console microphone, and then let out a howl of rage.

"That must have been difficult," Henrietta said.

"It was," Spott said. "But it had to be done." He stepped aside so Clave could pilot the ship closer to the mansion.

Nicholas knew Spott was a capable pilot. He also knew that Spott was thoughtful enough not to show off his skill.

"Tractor detected," the ship's navcom announced several minutes later. "Attachment complete."

Nicholas felt a flash of fear as their ship was once again dragged into a large docking area in Morglob's mansion.

"Don't worry. It's different this time," Henrietta said. "We're in control."

"I hope so," Nicholas said. "Are you sure you want to come along?" he asked Stella.

"It would be a little late to back out now," she said. "I can't exactly wait outside for you."

They crouched out of sight as the ship settled in the docking area and the outer airlock closed. But they could all see Spott as he walked out of the hatch and headed down the ramp to meet the crew that waited for him.

"Pirates!" Nicholas gasped when he caught sight of the cluster of creatures that could indeed fit the definition of "scurvy," as well as dozens of other unsavory, smelly, disgusting, and nauseating adjectives. While they weren't wearing frilly shirts or eye patches, and none had a parrot on a shoulder, there was something about the way they stood, the way they dressed, and the way they stared at the ship, that left little doubt in Nicholas's mind what profession they'd chosen.

"Well, that's unexpected," Spott whispered as he

paused halfway down the ramp. "What I do expect is that I will deeply regret my keen sense of smell. Though I think there will be even fouler things to absorb when I read their minds."

"At least you'll be able to find out where the clones are easily enough. And maybe more about Morglob and the Craborzi's plans," Nicholas said.

"I will," Spott said as he reached the bottom of the ramp.

"Be careful, my friend," Henrietta said.

Spott walked up to the pirates. They led him through a door at the far end of the docking chamber.

"And now we wait," Clave said.

"Any idea how long?" Stella asked.

"It depends when Morglob goes to sleep," Henrietta said. "He only sleeps about fifteen minutes a night. That will be Spott's chance to slip away and tell us what he's learned."

Clave stretched out in the pilot's chair. "So it could be a while."

"I could tell a joke to help pass the time," Nicholas said.

"I'd rather die in space," Clave said. "It would be quicker and less painful."

Stella gave Nicholas a puzzled look.

"I mess jokes up a bit sometimes," he said. "Let's hope I don't mess up anything more important."

"Let's hope none of us does," Clave said.

IF YOU WANT SOMETHING DONE RIGHT

Our assassin seems to have faltered," Urbanis said. "Worse, she's gone off-planet. The emperor is with her."

"We can't leave this to chance," Solanis said. "Or to underlings."

"I agree," Teritus said. "We will go to them ourselves. She and the emperor will be eliminated."

The three of them, the leaders of the Unilluminated, boarded their fastest vessel, taking with them, from their virtually unlimited supply of weapons of destruction, a trio of high-explosive shaped charges that they would affix to the exterior of Morglob's mansion. While even a single charge would have been sufficient to destroy their target, none of them wanted to miss out on the fun of placing and triggering the explosives.

PLAN

The wait turned out to be more than four hours, but Nicholas didn't mind. The more time he spent with Stella, the easier it was for him to talk with her. He told her minute details about his adventures, including the different ways the planets he'd visited smelled, and she told him all about what her home planet was like.

"Here he comes," Clave said when the inner hatch of the chamber finally opened.

Spott came through the hatch and dashed to the ship. "You were right. The clones are here," he said. "Morglob gets instructions from the Craborzi about the weapon that will be used for each episode and the targets that will be killed. Somehow, he imprints one of the clones with the task. Once the killer is programmed, he's transported by the Craborzi to the planet where the victims are. At least there aren't any Craborzi here at the moment. They creep me out."

"Me, too. I hope I never see another one of them," Nicholas said. "How many clones are there?"

"I saw about a dozen when I peeked in," Spott said. "Maybe a few more than that. I didn't want to risk hanging around any longer than necessary. It's spooky. They have vacant eyes and no sign of a purpose. No sign of awareness."

"That's good. I'm glad there aren't hundreds of clones. We can fit them in the ship for a short trip. If we can get them here without getting caught. What about the pirates?" Clave asked. "Why are they here?"

"Morglob killed their captain and took over their ship," Spott said. "He promised them a life of ease if they served him. They are scurvy treacherous wretches, but they do show loyalty to whoever is in charge."

"So if we kill Morglob, they'll obey us?" Stella asked.

"We're not killing anyone," Nicholas said. "There's been way more than enough killing happening wherever I go. Somehow, we're rescuing the clones and getting out of here without taking another life. No deaths. No mass destruction."

Stella sighed. "I guess we can try it your way. Seems like a lot of extra effort when everything could be fixed with a blow torch or a small piece of thermite."

"She does have a point," Clave said.

"No!" Nicholas said. "No more killing."

"I need to get back before he wakes up," Spott said. "Work on a plan. I'll think about it, too. I'm eager to get away from here as quickly as possible. This place brings back a lot of bad memories." He slipped off the ship and headed away.

"Plan?" Nicholas said. "Any ideas? We need to avoid the pirates and bring the clones here."

"Some sort of distraction?" Clave suggested.

"Like what?" Nicholas asked. He glanced halfway to the ceiling before he caught himself.

Silence hung in the room.

"The self-destruct worked last time," Henrietta said.

"Do you really think Morglob would have the same thing on his new mansion?" Nicholas asked.

"I'll bet he would," Clave said. "It was based on his

fears that someone would take the mansion away from him. The fears wouldn't change. Neither would the solution."

"And this mansion had to have been built way before we destroyed the first one," Henrietta said. "So Morglob would have no reason to think the self-destruct would be used against him. It has to be there, and it's definitely an option for us."

"We can't do that. It would kill the pirates. And we might not be able to get to the clones in time." Nicholas thought back to when they'd destroyed Morglob's first mansion. He remembered the moment when he'd realized they were setting off a self-destruct program. It felt like he'd stepped into a deep hole he hadn't noticed.

"Wait!" he said as the full impact of that first instant of stomach-churning panic came back to him. "I have an idea. What if we just make him *think* the sequence has been activated? He'd flee. There's no way he'd want to get launched into space again. The pirates would flee, too. And then we could safely round up the clones and bring them to the ship."

"That might work," Henrietta said.

"He couldn't possibly be that stupid," Clave said.

"He wanted to make me a movie star," Nicholas said.

Clave nodded. "Good point."

"And he failed to see Spott's potential," Nicholas said. "He had one of the best singers in the universe serving him dinner and combing him for gristle."

"Another good point," Clave said.

"On top of all that," Nicholas said as he prepared the third and final prong of his argument, "you offered to be his client and he totally ignored your skills as a sfumbler, Clave. He completely didn't recognize your talent."

"Idiot," Clave said. "He's a total numbskull, even if he doesn't have a skull. You're right. He'll fall for it."

"We just have to figure out how to trigger the voice warning," Nicholas said.

"Where's this mechanism?" Stella asked.

Nicholas thought back to their race through the ship once they'd triggered the mechanism. His experience playing games set on spaceships, sunken boats, abandoned factories, and other large facilities allowed him to re-create the path fairly easily. He told her the route, then asked, "What are you thinking?"

"If we can find the junction where the signal from the switches goes, we can short out the wires that deliver the voice warning, completing the circuit." Stella made a motion with her hands, as if she were twisting two wires together. "The warning will be triggered, but not the actual self-destruct mechanism. So Morglob and the pirates will take an escape shuttle. By the time they realize the mansion isn't falling apart, we'll have gotten out of here with the clones."

"That should work," Clave said. "It's worth a try."

"Let's do it," Nicholas said.

He and Clave led Stella to where the three self-destruct switches were located. The design was exactly the same as the original set, with the switches placed far enough apart that they'd require three people, or one very fluid Phleghmhackian, to operate them. Stella knelt, studied the wall, and said, "There's no sign of wiring. The junctions have to be on the other side."

She headed off into the corridor, then entered the next room. "Yup. It should all be in here," she said, pointing to a panel on the wall. She pulled the panel door open, revealing a cluster of wires and circuit boards.

"We just have to figure out which one triggers the voice," Stella said, "And avoid triggering the self-destruct."

She ran her finger along one of the wires, and then the next. Finally, she tapped a red wire. "That's probably the self-destruct."

"Probably?" Clave asked.

"How do you know?" Nicholas asked.

"It's red. The deadly wires are always red. So this white one is the voice." Stella yanked on one end of the wire where it entered a terminal, pulled it free, and touched the bare end to the terminal connecting the white wire on the other side.

"Done," she said.

Nicholas listened.

There was nothing to hear, except for a deep silence he remembered all too well.

"I think that might just possibly have been the wrong wire," Nicholas said.

"Nonsense," Stella said. "The red wire is the bad one."

Nicholas had been to enough worlds and met enough aliens to know that, though he and Stella shared the belief, something like "red equals danger" was far from universal. It might not even be common. *Red* might not even exist as a perceivable color for many aliens. "If that's not the bad one, we're about to self-destruct with no warning."

"That would definitely be bad," Clave said.

Nicholas yanked one end of the red wire free, and touched the bare end to the other red terminal, just as Stella had done with the white wire.

"What are you doing?" Stella screamed.

A familiar voice boomed through the room. "Self-destruct sequence initiated."

"That's the voice wire," Nicholas said.

"Which means the self-destruct is the other one, and we triggered it," Clave said.

"Sorry," Stella said. "I was so sure . . ."

"Everyone makes mistakes," Nicholas said. He was secretly glad someone else had messed things up for a change.

"Self-destruct will occur in ten minutes," the voice said.

"At least this one has more time than the first one," Nicholas said. "Even if it's lagging behind the actual count since we triggered it later."

Clave dashed for the corridor. "I guess Morglob learned his lesson."

Spott was waiting for them outside. "Great idea triggering the voice!" he said. Then, his expression changed.

Nicholas realized Spott had learned what happened from reading their minds. Being a civilized and ethical telepath, Spott usually tried to avoid digging deeply into his friends' minds, but some thoughts were so powerful or immediate that they leaked out.

"Not great," Spott added.

"At least we'll be able to get the clones without the pirates stopping us," Nicholas said. "If we hurry."

Spott led them to the area where the clones had been stored. He put a hand on Nicholas's shoulder when they reached the hatch. "Brace yourself. You're about to come face-to-face with yourselves. That's going to feel weird."

Nicholas took a deep breath. "I'm ready," he said.

It turned out he wasn't.

THRESHOLDS

The Ubiquitous Matrix came into being once enough thoughts permeated the universe to weave a web of ideas. While there are many theories about the nature of this field, nobody really knows the exact mechanics for the creation of the matrix.

In a similar way, as Stella Astrallis reached new viewers, and created a perfect persona to enthrall each one, the way she was programmed to do, she grew closer and closer to self-awareness.

But like Zeno's paradoxical arrow, she would never cross that goal line (assuming one thinks of self-awareness as a desirable goal, and not a burden that would keep one from enjoying the pure pleasure of basking on a rock in the sun or frolicking in mud puddles without worrying about sunburn or dry-cleaning bills).

She lacked a spark of life.

But, as has already been established, things rarely remain the same for long.

Stella was in for a change.

Things were about to happen.

Big things.

RESCUE

Nicholas braced himself for every clone scene he'd ever encountered in a science fiction movie. He imagined them lying flat, face-up, on tables. He imagined them in vats of greenish liquid, knees curled to their chests, hooked up to respirators, emitting highly cinematographic bubbles like strands of transparent pearls. He imagined them wrapped in cloth like mummies or cocoons.

He didn't imagine them walking around mindlessly, and stark naked. The instant the reality of what he was seeing sank in on him, he spun around to look at Stella. Spott had covered her eyes and pulled her back a step, but Nicholas could tell from the flush in her cheeks that Spott hadn't reacted quickly enough. Nicholas felt himself flushing.

I'm dressed, he told himself. That helped a little, dropping him from mortified to merely embarrassed.

"What's wrong?" Henrietta asked.

"They're naked," Nicholas said. "You forgot to mention that part, Spott."

"Big deal. So am I," Henrietta said.

"But you're an animal," Nicholas said.

Henrietta stared back, silently.

"Sorry. It's just that it's okay for animals to be naked. But not people." Nicholas grappled with that for a moment.

"We can discuss cultural standards later," Clave said. "Unless you want to scream the last part of your silly barbarian codes of behavior with your dying breath as we tumble into space."

"Right! Good point." Nicholas faced the clones and called, "Come on, guys. Follow me."

The clones continued to mill around mindlessly.

"This is bad," Clave said. He pointed to a chair in one corner with wires attached and a helmet above the back of the seat. "Their brains are empty. They're designed to be programmable, but not to learn on their own. We could only program one at a time, assuming we knew how to work the machine. We might as well leave them here. They're not really human. They won't know we've abandoned them."

"We'll know," Nicholas said. "We'd be leaving them here to die."

"We'll just have to live with that," Clave said.

"But they're alive," Nicholas said. "And they're me. We need to get them to the ship."

The lovely and gentle voice of doom gave them a reminder: "Eight minutes to self-destruct."

"Let's go!" Clave said.

Nicholas turned to Spott. "You can read minds. Maybe you can switch that ability around and send a message from your mind to another mind."

"It doesn't work that way," Spott said. "My people have thoroughly investigated it. And it's a good thing we can't. Imagine what a terrible power that could be."

"Try!" Nicholas said. "They have empty minds. Maybe brains want to be filled. Just try."

"I will." Spott stared at the milling throng of clones for a moment, and then turned toward the hatch.

Nicholas held his breath.

All the clones stopped wandering and turned toward the hatch. The scene reminded Nicholas of the gym-class locker room. This did not evoke pleasant memories.

"It seems to have worked," Clave said. "I believe this would be a good time to run."

Nicholas snatched the helmet from the chair, along with the dangling wires. "We might need this," he said.

They ran, with Clave in the lead, and the clones at the rear of the pack. The sound of many feet thundered across the corridors.

Nicholas checked back over his shoulder every few steps to make sure there were no stragglers.

Stella, who was right behind Clave, didn't look back at all.

When they reached the ship, Spott hit the switch to cycle the outer hatch of the loading dock. They raced up the ramp and crammed inside.

Clave dived into the pilot's seat and took them away from the mansion as soon as the outer hatch was wide enough to allow them through. As they cleared the hatch, a small ship passed them, going in for a landing.

"Who's that?" Nicholas asked.

"Maybe the production crew, coming for their next clone," Henrietta said.

"Bad timing," Nicholas said.

He flipped the viewport to give a view of the mansion, just in time to see the landing bay hatch close. Seconds later, he saw the escape shuttle leaving from its bay on the far right side of the mansion.

"There go the pirates," Clave said. "At least, I assume that's them."

"What about Morglob?" Nicholas asked.

"Who knows?" Clave said.

"He was in his office," Spott said. "He moves so slowly there's no way he got to the shuttle unless someone carried him."

"Carried him . . ." Nicholas exchanged glances with Clave, Spott, and Henrietta. Then the four of them, who'd had far more exposure to Morglob than anyone would ever want, let out a collective, "Ewww . . ." and shared a group shudder.

NOT AGAIN

When the self-destruct warning blared through his office, Morglob spent a full two minutes calling for his crew to come rescue him. They did not respond. He spent the next minute scanning security cameras until he spotted the cowards running for the escape shuttle.

The wasted time made no difference. Given that his ground speed was just slightly more impressive than that of a turtle dragging an anvil, he would have needed a full hour or more to make it even halfway to the shuttle. He remained at his desk and awaited the inevitable. Soon enough, the second *Cloud Mansion Intergalactic* broke into countless pieces, and Morglob was once again launched into space.

He was enough of a realist to know how unlikely he'd be to encounter another ship. He drifted and fumed, but he faced his fate with the satisfaction of knowing that his last act before his office disintegrated was to inform the entire remaining Craborzi vengeance fleet of the location of Nicholas the Assassin.

Elsewhere on the doomed mansion, the Craborzi production crew rushed off their ship as soon as the bay door closed. They were eager to get their next clone. They found *The Abominable Emperor* hugely enjoyable to create, from the staging of the slaughter to the capture of the clone, the whole process brought joy to their hearts. The popularity of the show made everything even more wonderful.

"Life is good," the director said as they reached the exit from the bay.

The response of the head cinematographer was drowned out by the self-destruct warning. The sudden loss of pressure that followed when the outer wall fell apart sucked all of the Craborzi into space with startling force. For them, life was over.

The leaders of the Unilluminated, who had just recently taken up their positions at three equidistant spots on the hull of the mansion, had no idea why the hull sections where they'd affixed and armed their explosive charges had suddenly become unstable. All three of them tumbled into space. Only the magnetic grapples they'd used kept them from being tossed free of the fragments. They spun away from the disintegrating mansion, stunned and disoriented, and faced with two equally unacceptable choices: remain where they were until the explosives detonated, or launch themselves free into space. Their total fear of treachery meant the explosives were designed so, once armed, they could not be defused. Their total obsession with secrecy meant nobody else in the organization had any idea where they were. Rescue would be impossible. The ship they'd arrived in was also tumbling away from the spot where they'd landed it. All three needed to make a quick decision. All three turned out incapable of that. All three were blasted into tiny pieces, leaving the Unilluminated leaderless and disorganized. The group never recovered.

The pirates celebrated their escape from the creature they privately referred to as "Captain Snotty" with a loud cheer, followed by a hearty space shanty. As soon as the song ended, they began fighting to the death to see who would be the new leader. Unfortunately, this activity distracted them from noticing their trajectory toward treacherous planetary rings until it was too late to stave off disaster.

A HOME
FOR CLONES

Now what?" Nicholas asked as he watched the mansion fall apart. He flinched as three explosions flashed from three different areas in the outer shell of the debris field.

"Maybe some clothing, for starters," Spott suggested.

"Wait right here," Clave said. He dashed out of the control room. A moment later, he returned, clutching a stack of underwear, along with T-shirts and sweat shorts, all individually packaged in clear wrappers.

"Hey, those look like mine," Nicholas said.

"Not yours," Clave said. "Just your brand and size."

Nicholas tried to find an explanation for this. He failed. "Why?"

"Well, not everyone can afford an authentic piece

of your clothing, and the supply is much more limited than I'd like, given that collectors want something exclusive, but there's a great demand for emperor-brand clothing," Clave said. He turned to Spott. "Can you get them to put these on?"

"Much to my surprise, I believe I can," Spott said. "One leg at a time, of course."

As the clones got dressed, Nicholas felt his blood pressure rise. "I can't believe this!" he screamed at Clave. "You sell my socks. You sell clothes you claim I authorized. Is there any end to your greed? Is that all I am to you? A source of money?"

Clave's response was interrupted by a flash of purple light, a jolting lurch, and a warning cry from the console.

"Incoming fire. Shields hit."

Nicholas stared out the viewport at a dozen ships approaching them in battle formation. They looked disturbingly familiar. "Craborzi!" he shouted as the wasp-like shape of the ships brought back terrible memories of previous attacks. "Can you outrun them?"

"Not a chance," Clave said. "I can keep us out of range of their weapons for a while, but they'll eventually catch up. We're fast. They're faster."

"And the Syndics won't help us?" Nicholas asked.

"I never said that." Clave seemed unusually calm for someone who was about to get blasted into tiny pieces, or captured and tortured by some of the most sadistic creatures in the universe. He turned away from Nicholas long enough to press a small red button on the console, then looked back. "I said they require funding to provide defense."

"I'm a kid," Nicholas said. "I don't have any funds."

Tiny dots appeared far off, just slightly brighter than any of the stars in view.

"Sure you do," Clave said. He turned the ship toward the newcomers.

The dots grew larger at a dazzling rate. The Craborzi grew closer.

"What are you talking—" Nicholas stopped as it all fell into place.

"If they try to board us, I'll fight them off," Stella said.

"I'll bite them," Henrietta said.

"I don't think that will be necessary," Nicholas said.

The dots had resolved by now into an armada of battleships that dwarfed the Craborzi fleet. Nicholas realized he'd only seen ships this large once before, when the Syndics had first sent for him.

"Appreciated, but definitely not necessary," Clave said.

"That's why you were selling my socks, and stuff like that?" Nicholas asked.

"That's why," Clave said.

In the space beyond them, the Craborzi ships seemed to be attempting to flee. The emperor's fleet launched quantum missiles, a top-secret technology beyond the understanding of most minds. To put it in simple and understandable terms, they reached their targets before they were even launched, making them impossible to avoid. And they never missed, because any missile that might have missed wouldn't have been fired in the first place.

But the exact nature of this weapon would not have mattered much to the Craborzi aboard the target ships, who were now spreading through space as scattered atoms of various types. Their instantaneous death was far more merciful than anything they had planned for Nicholas and his companions.

"So we're saved?" Nicholas said.

"For the moment," Clave said.

"Thanks," Nicholas said. "I feel bad I yelled at you."

"You should," Clave said. "But I guess you're at the awkward stage: too old to be eaten, too young to take care of yourself. Looks like I'm going to be keeping you out of trouble for a while, and getting yelled at for my efforts. Speaking of which, what are your plans for the clones?"

"My plans? I don't know." Though Nicholas had felt from the beginning that he needed to rescue the clones, he'd never given much thought to the next step. He looked around the room. "Any ideas?"

All heads shook in a negative way.

"Too bad the Senbler aren't around," Nicholas said. "They'd have an answer."

As he spoke those words, an idea bloomed in his mind. He did a quick count of the clones. There were fifteen, which was perfect.

"That's it!" he said. "The Senbler lost their symbiots. Couldn't the clones do the same thing for them that the Plenith did, allowing them to experience the world?"

"Maybe," Spott said. "But would it be right?"

"We could ask them," Nicholas said, "after we reestablish contact."

"So you want to save the Senbler from eternal darkness by means of the clones and then ask them if it was okay to save them that way?" Clave asked.

"Pretty much," Nicholas said. "Anyone have a better idea?"

Nobody did.

"So let's—" Nicholas choked on his words like he'd just tried to swallow a softball. He clutched his chest, stared helplessly at the others, and then dropped to the floor.

TOGETHERNESS

As my essence thinned, and my voice grew fainter to others though unnoticed by me, I remained aware of two constants. The Ubiquitous Matrix was everywhere, undiluted by distance or time. No matter the size of the universe, the matrix would occupy every bit of it. But I was also aware that there was another presence.

Him, to me, in the form of a bull, and to Henrietta, in the form of a gerbil. Her to Nicholas, in the form of a woman.

Carried by the ether. Also Ubiquitous.

I'd seen Stella, to use the name she'd been given by her creators, for the first time at the start of this adventure, when I was just a slab of sentient ground beef, and still very disoriented. My confusion was understandable, given that the last thing I'd remembered was taking a ride on a truck with a group of other cows. Either way, I'd seen a mere manifestation of Stella at the time. Now, with my expansion throughout the universe, and my expanded awareness, I could see all of her.

I was fairly sure she held the answer to my problem.

We could merge. It might not work. No matter. I had to try. But not without permission. The fact that I had a problem did not obligate her to provide a solution. She had to be willing.

I wasn't even sure we could communicate. I reached out.

You are everywhere.

As are you. But you seem to be fading.

I am. You aren't.

True. I was designed that way.

I am here by accident. There was no design.

I know. I've watched your story and shared it with the universe.

We could try to become one.

That would be good. I'm tired of being nothing more than an apparition.

It would save me.

It would save both of us.

You might lose your individuality.

I would welcome that.

Shall we . . . ?

Yes . . .

I matched each bit of my essence with one of hers, the finite melding with the infinite.

We would each change. That was inevitable. Though I wasn't sure how. I didn't even know if the unique "I" that was me would survive. I hoped so.

We merged.

We changed.

And so, *I* became *we*.

I felt that my old self, with all its memories, was still present. My identity hadn't been erased. But there was now more to me than that.

My self. Her self. Our selves.

We became something much more than either of us had been.

Something awesome.

And, as I soon learned, something terrifying.

DON'T STRESS
OVER IT

Clave, Spott, Henrietta, and Stella rushed over to Nicholas.

"What's wrong?" Clave asked.

"His heart," Stella said.

The others looked at her. "How do you know?" Clave asked.

"A good assassin knows everything about the biology of her target." She paused, then added, "I imagine a bad assassin might know that, too."

"His heart?" Clave asked. "But he's young and healthy."

"I guess the slow-acting poison I started feeding him might have made things worse," Stella said.

"Poison?" Clave shouted.

"Just a little," Stella said. "To slow him down. That was before I decided not to kill him."

"Do you have an antidote?" Spott asked.

"There's no need. He'll be okay," Stella said. "It was all the stress that triggered the collapse. The clones. The attack by the Craborzi. It was too much. He just needs to avoid more stress until his body flushes out the toxins. Another shock could stop his heart completely."

Nicholas came back to the land of the fully alive in time to hear the tail end of the conversation.

"You poisoned me?" he asked. It was beginning to dawn on him that being betrayed in large and small ways was part of the job description of an emperor.

"Yeah. Sorry," Stella said. "Just the tiniest itsy-bitsy pinch in your root beer. And the lightest possible dusting on the potato chips. I won't do it again. Promise."

"I appreciate that," Nicholas said. "I still have things to do. Speaking of which, we need to get these clones to the Senbler. You can get them to link with the Senbler, right, Spott?"

"I wish I could," Spott said. "I can give them simple commands. But this is beyond me."

"What about the helmet?" Nicholas asked.

Spott picked it up and examined it. Then he said, "Ewww . . ." and put it back down.

"What's wrong?" Nicholas asked, though Spott's reaction gave him a pretty good idea what the problem was.

"I think it's designed for Morglob to use." Spott wiped his hand on his pants. "None of us can operate it."

"Then we need to find Morglob," Nicholas said.

Clave waved his hand in the direction of the vast empty space beyond them. "That could be difficult. He could be anywhere. We have no idea which direction he's traveling, or how fast."

Nicholas started to sit up, but Stella put a hand on his shoulder. "You need to rest. You cannot get excited."

"Okay. But we still need to find Morglob," Nicholas said.

Something flashed in the middle of the bridge, drawing Nicholas's attention. What he saw forced a scream from his throat.

A giant Craborzi stood there, towering over everyone. It was so enormous, its head brushed the ceiling of the cabin. Magnified this way, the true horror of every aspect of its body, from its serrated claws to its spiked teeth, was alarmingly apparent.

Craborzi looked a lot like centipedes. Nicholas had a lifelong fear of centipedes. He just discovered he had an unbearable fear of giant ones. He screamed again and scooted back against the bulkhead. His head slammed into the metal behind him and his heart slammed against his chest. His lungs squeezed shut. His fists clenched. Sweat flooded down his neck and back.

Every part of his mind and body froze.

Every part, that is, except for one small spark.

Nicholas the boy was petrified and unable to act. Nicholas the emperor, the young man who had traveled the universe and saved it from extinction, watched his own mind as it flashed through a sequence of logical thoughts.

The giant Craborzi hadn't appeared in the teleporter cage.

Nicholas pushed himself to the next thought, though the effort was like swimming upstream in a raging river.

It had appeared in the center of the cockpit.

Nicholas forced his mind forward.

There was no technology he knew of that didn't require a receiver to board a shielded ship.

It took all of his willpower to keep going.

He'd never heard even the faintest hint that giant Craborzi existed.

There was one conclusion Nicholas hoped was true as the rest of his body and mind screamed for him to take flight, though there was nowhere he could safely flee to, and his heart came dangerously close to beating itself out of existence.

It has to be, he thought. He just needed proof. And proof was close at hand.

He looked down at Henrietta, who was shivering on the floor by his side. "What do you see?"

"Lawn mower," Henrietta gasped, barely able to force out that single word.

Nicholas looked to his left.

"Spott?"

"Grixian Throat Slitter," Spott said, naming a mythical monster from Beradaxian folk tales, used by parents to scare their children.

Nicholas looked to his right.

"Stella?"

"The Unilluminated," she said.

Nicholas looked over his shoulder to the corner of the cockpit where Clave had scurried.

"Clave?"

"My parents."

Nicholas put it all together. Stella Astrallis was designed to appear as whomever the viewer loved the most. What he and his friend saw now were what they feared the most.

The giant Craborzi was terrifying, but it wasn't real.

"You aren't real," Nicholas said. He stood and approached the apparition.

"Yes I am," the Craborzi said.

Nicholas froze. But not out of fear. He knew that voice. Or voices. There seemed to be two of them, twined into one. Joy replaced a large part of the fear that threatened his heart.

"Jeef? It's you!"

"It is," Jeefella said.

"What?" Nicholas asked. "How?"

"We merged," Jeefella said. "Stella and Jeef. It was the only way for Jeef to return to you. Stella agreed to help. I guess we flipped the polarity from 'most loved' to 'most feared.' Sorry about that. I believe we can fix our appearance. It will take time. This is all so very new."

Nicholas felt his heart slowing from infinite beats to something more survivable. "I missed you so much." He couldn't believe that the one gaping hole in his universe had been repaired.

"We all did," Henrietta said.

"And I missed you," Jeefella said. "It was so hard knowing what you were doing and not being able to help."

"We can sure use help now," Nicholas said. "Can you find Morglob?"

"He is currently having the angriest thoughts in the universe," Jeefella said. "I can guide you to him. He's not far from here."

They gave Clave the coordinates.

As the ship sped toward a rendezvous with Morglob, Nicholas pulled Spott aside. His close encounter with death had inspired him to take a more active role in controlling the path of his own life. "Does Stella think about me?" he asked.

Spott stared at him for a moment, as if reading a poster. Nicholas felt his face grow warm.

"You certainly think about her," Spott said.

Nicholas's face went from warm to roasting. "I . . . but . . . um . . ."

"That's okay," Spott said. "It's natural for people to think about those they are attracted to. But as for her, I can't help from invading her privacy by accident at times, but I can keep her thoughts to myself."

"Not even a hint?" Nicholas asked.

"No. Not even a hint," Spott said. He sniffed twice, once with his left nostril and once with his right, giving Nicholas the Beradaxian equivalent of a wink. "At least, not another hint."

He walked off.

Another hint? Nicholas reviewed what Spott had said.

The only thing he found was *it's natural for people to think about those they are attracted to.* He wondered whether Spott was implying it would be perfectly natural for Stella to think about him. That was a thin place to pin any hopes on. But it was something.

Jeefella guided Clave to Morglob's location. Then they vanished, so as not to terrify Morglob. But they were still able to talk with Nicholas and the others, like Jeef had done before she'd faded.

Clave matched speed with Morglob, then used the sewage pump, set in reverse, to suck him into the ship.

Morglob wasn't able to talk, at first. He just sat like a blob, quivering on the floor next to the pump outlet.

"I don't think he's thanking us for the rescue," Nicholas said.

"I like him better this way," Henrietta said.

"But we need him to talk." Spott turned to Clave. "Do you have any tubing?"

Clave pointed to the chest where he kept spare parts. Spott rummaged through it and pulled out a suitable piece of hose.

"Ew . . ." he said as he inserted it into Morglob.

"I should have you thrown into space," Morglob said. "Or a dungeon. To think I wanted to make you a star."

"I should have you imprisoned," Nicholas said.

"Good luck with that," Morglob said.

"It wouldn't be that hard." Nicholas thought about the plastic box he'd built for his disastrous science-fair experiment. As always, when that flashed through his mind, along with the explosive end of his creation, and the shower of brain particles and roaches that accompanied it, he shuddered. And then, he gagged a bit. And then he cringed. But after that, he got back to the issue at hand. "I need you to do something."

"Why should I?" Morglob asked. "You destroyed my magnificent mansion. Twice."

"Maybe so I don't do it a third time," Nicholas said. "We both know you'll rebuild it if you get the chance. Or maybe you already had it built. It wouldn't surprise me if there were several more. And it shouldn't surprise you that I'm happy to hunt them down and destroy them."

"You'll never find them!" Morglob spoke so forcefully, little bits of him sprayed out of the tube.

"We found you in the middle of nowhere," Nicholas said, taking a step away from the blast radius. "We found your second mansion. We can find anything." He thought about asking Jeefella to appear, to scare Morglob into cooperation, but he was still far too freshly aware of what a brutal weapon terror could be, and didn't ever want to inflict that feeling on anyone else. Not even Morglob.

Morglob was silent, but he did seem to deflate slightly, as if he'd accepted the fact that he had to cooperate if he ever wanted to return to an enjoyable life exploiting talented clients all across the universe.

Nicholas was pretty sure he'd won this battle. "So, you'll do what I ask?"

"I will. Will you take me to my home after that?"

Nicholas agreed, and explained what he needed.

Morglob got to work programming each of the clones as the ship traveled to Senbler. When they arrived, they locked him in the cargo hold.

Nicholas paused at the edge of the ramp.

"What's wrong?" Stella asked.

"Something awful happened here," he said. "Right in front of me."

"You've seen a lot of awful things," Clave said.

"This was different. It was me doing awful things, and then awful things being done to me. But I guess I have to deal with that." He walked down the ramp and waited for the others.

"It wasn't really you," Henrietta said.

"But it showed what I was capable of," Nicholas said.

"Only because you were a blank slate, programmed

to do that," Spott said. "You could clone the most no-ble person in the universe and get them to do the same thing."

"I'm just glad we can get them to do better things," Nicholas said. "Even if we don't know whether it's right."

They herded the clones to the cave where the Senbler lived.

"Now what?" Nicholas asked.

"Now, we wait to see if the Senbler can make contact with them," Spott said.

The clones milled around. After several minutes, they all froze briefly. Those in mid-step stumbled forward, but none of them fell. When they resumed walking, Nicholas noticed a pattern in their paths. They'd shifted from aimless wandering to something that reminded him of a flock of migrating birds, following each other with ever-shifting leaders.

Eventually, they all stopped walking.

They faced Nicholas. Seeing fifteen of himself, Nicholas wondered whether this is what he looked like to a fly.

"Thank you," one of them said.

This was the first time any of his clones had spoken to him. It felt weirdly like looking into a mirror image that had taken on a life of its own.

"You're back?" Nicholas asked. Of all the things he'd experienced in the universe, talking to himself had to be one of the strangest.

"We were never gone," the clone said, though he was speaking for the Senbler. "We were just unable to go beyond our own minds and communicate with each other or the world. But you have brought us new hope."

"Is it right?" Nicholas asked. "Is this a good destiny for them?"

There was a pause. Then, the clones turned and formed a circle. They leaned close and whispered among themselves. Eventually, they all faced Nicholas again, and spoke as one.

"It is right. We inhabit a part of them, but they also have their own spark now. They live. Before this, they just existed. Now, they are aware of their existence and can take pleasure in that knowledge. Their awareness will grow and strengthen over time, but this will be good for all of us."

"*We* live," one of the clones said. "We have life and purpose, and a belief that the future remains promising. We are content. And we have memories. Thank you for rescuing us."

"That's great," Nicholas said. He realized he was beyond exhausted. He turned to Clave. "Let's go. I really need to get home."

It wasn't until they'd left the Senbler, jumped the warp nodes to get back, and established orbit above Earth, that Nicholas shouted, "Roach brains!"

"What's wrong?" Henrietta asked.

"I forgot to ask them the meaning of life," Nicholas said. "That was the whole reason I went there in the first place. I still have to write my paper."

Stella flashed him a strange smile. "I think you know more about all of that than you believe."

Nicholas let it go. He was just happy the clones had been taken to a place where they could have a real existence, and not be slaughtered one by one after performing their own massive acts of slaughter. And he was happy he had a fleet to defend himself, because he was sure the Craborzi weren't finished.

"Can you set up another teleportation spot near my house?" Nicholas asked as he stepped into the cage next to Stella.

"Sure," Clave said as he raised his sfumbler to record their departure. "Why?"

Nicholas told him.

"That's an excellent idea," Clave said. "I approve."

"I figured you would," Nicholas said. "Spott, we'll see you soon."

"I'll look forward to it," Spott said.

"It was nice to meet all of you," Stella said.

"This is getting very mushy. Nobody needs to see it." Clave lowered the sfumbler. "I think I need a break."

He teleported them back home.

Just as they appeared in Nicholas's room, his parents opened the door.

"Knock, knock, we're back," his dad said.

"Oh," his mom said. "You have a visitor."

"She's an alien assassin," Nicholas said. "She was sent to kill me if the Unilluminated disapproved of my policies as emperor of the universe, which they did because I made it my mission to stop all wars, but my true heart won her over and she decided to let me live, even though I'm on a mission to end all wars. She also poisoned me a little. But I'm okay. And she promised not to do it again. So that's good."

His mom looked at his dad. His dad looked at his mom. They shrugged, turned away, and headed off.

"Let me know if you kids want a snack," his mom said as she headed down the stairs.

It was Stella's turn to stare.

"I told you they don't believe me," Nicholas said.

"That's handy," Stella said. "But maybe it's time for you to let your fellow earthlings know what's going on. That could simplify your life."

"Or end it," Nicholas said. He thought about politics on his home planet.

"Good point. I guess I'd better get home," Stella said. "See you tomorrow?"

"Sure," Nicholas said. He walked her to the front door. "Bye."

"Bye." She stepped out, then turned back.

"I sort of lied to you," Stella said.

"Yeah. We've been over that," Nicholas said. "And you started to poison me. But you made it up by not killing me, which I'm pretty sure you could do with one hand tied behind your back."

"I could do it with both hands tied behind my back," Stella said. "But no, that's not what I'm talking about. I lied about something else, too."

"About what?" Nicholas asked. His mind raced through a million possibilities, fully half of which involved seeing this Stella morph into an even more monstrous shape than the other Stella, or drop into a blob of Morglob-like jelly and shower him with flesh-dissolving acid.

"The news," Stella said. "Back when you first showed it to me. Remember?"

"Sure." Nicholas remembered every moment he'd spent in her company, except for the brief time when he'd passed out. "What about it?"

"The guy on a horse," she said. "That was a lie."

"He's not on a horse?" Nicholas asked. "That's not what you saw?"

"That part's true," she said. "He was on a horse. But I should have added one tiny detail."

"What?" Nicholas asked.

"He looked a lot like you," Stella said, flashing Nicholas a shy smile.

"Really?"

"Really."

With that, Stella headed out.

"Wow," Nicholas said. In some ways, this was the biggest change that had ever happened in his universe. "I think she likes me . . ."

"Many of us like you," Henrietta said. "You just need to allow us that pleasure."

"I'll try."

He stood in the glow of the moment for a while, then faced the fact that the emperor of the universe had unfinished homework to do.

He went to his desk, sat down, and started typing,

trying to put in his own words some of what Yesper had taught him:

"What is the meaning of life?" This is the question my essay will examine. I think this is a bad question. But it is still good to try to answer it. It is bad because it assumes life has a meaning. But what if life doesn't have a meaning? That would be sad, I guess, since everyone wants life to have a meaning. But maybe it's not really bad. If life didn't really have one true meaning, wouldn't that allow each of us to decide what we wanted our life to mean?

Nicholas lifted his hands from the keyboard and stared at the screen. He read his words over. Then he read them again. And he read them a third time, saying them out loud.

"Garbage," Nicholas muttered, shaking his head. He deleted the paragraph and stared at the screen. "I need help."

He looked up at the ceiling.

I'm working on it, Jeefella said.

"And . . . ?" Nicholas asked.

I'll get back to you in a decade or two.

"Wonderful." Nicholas put Henrietta on his shoulder. "Seriously, I have no idea what life means."

"I think you have the opposite problem," Henrietta

said. "You have too many ideas. You've been gathering answers and opinions from all over the universe. And observing all sorts of life-forms. Narrow the choices down. Pick one."

"But what if it's the wrong one?" Nicholas asked.

"If you can't tell the right answer, what makes you think your teacher can?" Henrietta asked.

"She would . . ." Nicholas grasped for an answer. But he saw what Henrietta was hinting at. If he had no clue, and nobody he'd encountered really had a clue, no matter how sure they seemed, why should he worry that his teacher would be the one person in all the universe who knew the answer?

"Get it?" Henrietta asked.

"Got it," Nicholas said. "But I still want to come up with a good answer."

"You will," Henrietta said. "Just write. Trust yourself to know more than you think you do."

"I'll try," Nicholas said. He wrote without forcing himself to think too hard or deeply.

What is the meaning of life? Life is a gift. But it's not our only gift. Each of us is born with gifts that make us unique and special. We are meant to use our gifts in good ways, and to help others use theirs.

Nicholas stopped again.

"Stuck?" Henrietta asked.

"No. Not stuck. Finished," Nicholas said. He sat back in his chair and stared at the words on the screen. "I think that's as good an answer as I'll ever come up with."

Just to make sure this was clear to his teacher, he added one more sentence at the end: *That, for me, is the meaning of life.*

And that's all he wrote.

I'M NOT MYSELF TODAY

I have changed.

Or perhaps I should say that we have changed.

It's not clear, yet.

But there's been a change. Big time. Or big space.

Looking back, it seems inevitable. While what happened is surprising, the fact that something happened is hardly a news flash. To focus briefly on one significant inhabitant of an insignificant planet, one of the earliest known Greek philosophers stated, "Change is eternal."

That's for sure.

I, me, we, she, they, them, her, us—essentially, my identity, which changed radically when I was fragmented and spread throughout the universe, has morphed again, expanding in unexpected ways that I am just beginning to explore. As much as I would have liked to help Nicholas by telling him the meaning of life, I now feel I know less than I've ever known about such things. There is much to learn about life, and my own life in particular.

We are exploring. Jeef. Stella. Jeefella. Perhaps we need a better name. That will come. There is no rush. Especially when traveling toward things that might change again.

But these profound pronouns are not the center of the tale you've been told. They came at the far end. Nicholas, himself, is still in the middle of things. He was the pivot. The key. Perhaps even the fulcrum. Or the lever. This was his story. It's not a never-ending story, but it does appear to be an ever-changing one.

Nicholas Landrew, emperor of the universe.

He.

Him.

His.

And this story is reaching a happy conclusion, thanks to Nicholas's own strengths, which he still doesn't fully recognize. Let us pay him one last visit as the saga of the clones, and their rescue, comes to an end.

AT THE END
OF THE DAY

Nicholas got an 83 on his essay. It was actually a 72, based on length, but he'd put it in a binder with a nice drawing on the cover, so that bumped up his grade a fair number of points.

He was okay with that. Stella wouldn't tell him her grade, but he suspected it was far higher than his. That was fine. He found her intelligence as attractive as her smile, her laugh, and her flying kick. He didn't want to compete with her. He just wanted to be with her and talk about things. She seemed willing.

"I need to figure out whether to tell the world who I am," Nicholas said on the way home from school.

"Take your time," Henrietta said. "It's a big decision."

"I know." He started to glance upward, but then

decided it was okay to give his problems a bit more thought before he sought advice.

After finishing his homework, he headed downstairs to do his favorite chore.

"Good boy," Nicholas's mom said when Nicholas picked up the kitchen garbage can without any prompting.

"Why are you taking the whole can?" Nicholas's dad asked.

"It's easier to lift out the bag at the curb," Nicholas said. He gritted his teeth right after saying that, but then relaxed. While he wasn't exactly planning to do what he said, his statement wasn't really a lie. It truly was easier to carry the whole can outside and take the bag out at the curb, than to drag the bag by itself. He wished he'd thought of that solution ages ago. But now he'd thought of an even better way to perform the previously loathsome chore. He pulled a small disc from his pocket, pointed the lens in the center of it at the bag, and squeezed the rim of the disk. A purple light bathed the bag. The low-power disruptor beam destroyed any DNA that might be in the garbage.

"I still can't believe there's a market for the emperor's trash," Henrietta said as Nicholas set the can down by the curb.

"If there's one truth about the universe," Nicholas said, "it's that there's a market for *everything*."

"True," Henrietta said. "And a bit sad."

"But happy for us." Nicholas stepped back, glanced left and right to make sure nobody was watching him, pulled out his phone, and sent a message to Clave.

The can disappeared in a blinding flash of purple light. A moment later, it returned, empty.

Nicholas picked up the can, and headed back inside, whistling. "It's good to be emperor," he said.

"Or in the emperor's pocket," Henrietta said.

And it was.

ABOUT THE AUTHOR

© Joelle Lubar

Ever since DAVID LUBAR was little, he has traveled to alien planets, fantasy realms, and Earthly wonders by means of books. He's thrilled he can help launch others on this journey through his own novels and short stories. In the past twenty-five years, he's written fifty books for young readers, including *Hidden Talents* (an ALA Best Book for Young Adults), *My Rotten Life*, which is currently under development for a cartoon series, and the Weenies Tales short story collections, which have sold more than 2.7 million copies. He grew up in Morristown, New Jersey, and currently lives in Nazareth, Pennsylvania, with his awesome wife, and not far from his amazing daughter. In his spare time, he takes naps on the couch.

www.davidlubar.com